THE BIG CHANCE . . .

"So, Diamond, your manager here tells me that you're one of the best-kept secrets around here."

"Yeah, well, I guess you could say that."

"Well," White laughs, "how about you let me judge that for myself?"

Michael's prompting me with hand gestures behind White. I have no idea what he expects me to do. Perform? He could've warned me or something.

Too late for all that, though. This is my big chance. I bust a rap into White's ear:

"Tap jaws and leave rap scarred / Make you ask / Has God? Pulled a fast card / When your brain is fracchawed / from the rapt-chaw / When I catch y'all . . ."

I'm building into a tempest when White shakes his head good-naturedly. "Only if you have a copy of your demo on you," he says. "I run into a lot of kids who can perform live but can't cut a decent record. I'm not a promoter—I don't sell shows. I sell albums."

"Well . . . I don't have my demo on me right now."

"But we can get it to you," Michael chimes in.

"Can you have it to my office by noon tomorrow?" White asks. "If you're as good as your manager here says you are, we might be able to do business."

Noon? Tomorrow? There is no f'n demo.

GHETTO SUPASTAR

GHETTO SUPASTAR

A novel by
Prakazrel "Pras" Michel
with kris ex

POCKET BOOKS
New York London Toronto Sydney Tokyo Singapore

ACKNOWLEDGMENTS

I would like to thank God, my family, Lennox and Lester Parris of The Parris Brothers, L.L.C., SONY, DAS Communications, Reza Isad, Guy Oseary, Darell D. Miller, Chris Hudson, and Cory Daniels.

An *Original* Publication of POCKET BOOKS

POCKET BOOKS, a division of Simon & Schuster Inc.
1230 Avenue of the Americas, New York, NY 10020

Copyright © 1999 by Prakazrel Michel

ISBN: 0-671-02730-1

First Pocket Books printing January 1999

10 9 8 7 6 5 4 3 2 1

POCKET and colophon are registered trademarks of Simon & Schuster Inc.

Cover designed by Brian Freeman
Cover photograph by Davis Factor

Printed in the U.S.A.

It is only in his music, which Americans are able to admire because a protective sentimentality limits their understanding of it, that the Negro in America has been able to tell his story.

—James Baldwin, *Notes of a Native Son*

Grabbed a book off the shelf / Put the thoughts on page / Slowed down the rage I felt when they got Gage / Took note of my age / 'Cause my shorty needs a new pair of Jordans, Wally's, and Timb's / A stroller with Perilli rims / A gold-plated jungle gym / And all that other shit that makes me K.I.M.

—Diamond St. James

"You *need* to do the cover of *InnaViews*," says my publicist, Jorge.

"They're the hottest music publication on the stands, Diamond," Jorge says. "Circulation eight hundred thousand. *Eight hundred thousand.* Do you know what that means, Diamond? They can take you to the next level. They really can."

Rosetta is standing in front of the range, playing with the oven's latch, twisting the knobs for the burners.

"Rosie!"

She gives me that look of innocent defiance. I swear I see her eyes roll when she turns back around.

"Rosie!" A bit angrier now.

She gives one knob a quick turn to the left.

Tek-tek-tek-tek-tek-tek-tek-tek-tek . . . The stovetop kicks out that incessant clicking, the pilot trying to ignite the burner.

"Ro—" I run, grab her, turn off the stove.

"Now why you gonna go and do that?"

Her tongue tips out through the space where her two front teeth used to be and she trembles on the inside of my elbow when she giggles.

I make like I'm angry by screwing up my face. "No," I say. She's her grandmother, able to see right through me. She smiles and flings up her arms to the ceiling for a hug.

Jorge is still talking when I get back to the receiver.

"Man, I don't know about doing any more press right now," I say. "A nigga's tired. And I definitely ain't doing *InnaViews*. I don't trust them motherfuckers as far as I can throw 'em."

"But the exposure, Diamond. Think about the exposure."

"Yeah—exposure. Just like they exposed Men of Sin. Nah, I don't trust them. It feels like a setup. They never checked for me before, why now?"

"A setup?" He laughs. "Diamond, I keep telling you that you really need to get off that ghetto mentality. You're a star now. You'd better start acting like one. And did you see Men of Sin's figures after that story came out? Through the roof, Diamond—through the freakin' roof. And besides, you don't have a three-year-old warrant for murder out on you. . . . Do you? I have it all set for next week. Tuesday, after the marketing meeting, we'll do the photo shoot. It'll probably take all day. They have Antione Cheraz for the shoot, Diamond. Antione Cheraz. He doesn't even do hip-hop artists. He's done Naomi, Tyra, Claudia . . ."

Rosetta is falling asleep in my lap. I should've

figured she was just tired and wanted a nest to lay in. Her fine strands of hair tickle my palm as I run my hand over her head.

"Poppy's not a killer," I whisper, kiss her on the forehead. "I never killed anyone who didn't deserve it."

". . . and cowboy boots. I think it's a great idea. What do you think?"

All I know is I ain't not taking no pictures looking like Wyatt Earp.

"Sounds, cool," I say. "But I have to hear it again."

"Okay. You're the Lone Ranger, a pioneer blazing new ground, a verbal gunslinger who shoots rhymes first and asks questions . . ."

A soft tone tells me that someone's on the other line. I click over without informing Jorge, 'cause I know he'll still be talking when I get back.

"You have a collect call from New York State Correctional Facility," the computerized voice says. "If you accept these charges, please press five or say yes at the tone. *Beep.*"

"Yes."

"Thank you," the impersonal voice says.

"Waddup, son?!"

"What's going on, nigga?"

"I'm on lockdown, what the fuck you think is going on?" says Michael.

There's a moment of silence, but I can hear him smiling on the other end.

"Man, don't make me have to take a trip up there and bust your ass on the next V.I."

He laughs that gruff, carefree laugh. "Man, you

need to get your ass up here. I ain't see you in weeks."

I laugh, happy to hear Michael happy. He's seventeen months into a twenty-five-to-life bid, but I don't think he realizes that yet, like he's in fierce denial. His mood usually switches from despair to anger like a pendulum. If he's not bitching, he sounds suicidal. He doesn't belong in there. Whatever his problems are, incarceration is only going to make them worse. No one comes from behind those walls whole.

"Yo, niggas up here is feeling that 'We Stay Quiet' joint."

"Say word. I'm a girl in high school who's just been told that the captain of the football team wants to take her to the prom."

"No word of a lie. Cats' feeling that shit. Everyone up here can relate to that joint."

They'd ask me about you and you about me / How could it be? / Wiped the prints from the gun / I stood firm 'cause I knew you couldn't run / You said, When they come through the door, let me be the only one / Best to be jetty, son / You got hopes and dreams, so you don't need to go down / There's bodies all over the ground / And two of them caught it from your four-pound / Break out before they come around / I said, Don't talk so much because when you do there's this funny sound / They took me in the back / Put you in the emergency truck / Bitch questioned me, but I kept my mouth shut / 'Cause I knew 'til your last breath you wasn't giving up fuck . . .

"Yo, you need to come up here and do a show. That shit would be off the hook!"

4

"True," I say. "But what's up? You keeping your head up?"

"Yeah. Some kid caught it in the mess hall last night over a carton of milk, though. Germans tore his chest the fuck open with a laundry hook. Shorty was getting down with Muslims, reading the Qur'an an' shit. Some Netas did it. You know, them Ali Baba motherfuckers ain't having it. They sharpenin' they scimitars right now. It's 'bout to be fuckin' Jihad out this bitch."

"Damn. You okay though?"

"C'mon, son. These niggas don't want no part of Gage. My name rings bells up here like Notre Dame."

I want to tell Michael that he's no longer in the streets. I want to tell him that he gotta watch his back; that I paid off three contracts on his life with the royalties and a few guest appearances on some wack rappers' albums.

"How Rosie?" he asks.

"She fine. She sleeping on my lap right now."

"That's hot, son. I know she gettin' all big an' shit. How old she is now?"

I want to answer, *How long you been in jail nigga?* "Seventeen months."

I can tell he's thinking about it.

"You got that commissary?" I ask.

"Yeah. Good lookin'."

"And them mix tapes?"

"No doubt, them shits is the bomb."

"And the magazines?"

"Yeah, yeah, yeah, I got all that shit," he waves me off with his words. The fire that he greeted me with is all but gone. "What I ain't got is a visit from my man. I know you busy and all, but try'n make your way up here."

We both stay silent for a minute. I hear a gang of vulgar conversations going on in the background. Someone's beefing about phone time. A C.O. is banging something wooden against something metal, telling everyone to quiet down, or else.

"Don't be forgettin' about me, son, " he says.

"Never that," I say. "Never that."

HALLELUJAH

Glistening streams of perspiration made their way down the Reverend Snider's face, into his eyes, nose, and mouth. He dabbed his carefully folded white cloth across his forehead.

"And the Lord said, 'I go to prepare a place for you.' Do you hear me brothers and sisters?" His voice bounced off the high ceilings in the small church and echoed over the din of the congregation's murmurs. Women fanned bulletins. The men, for the most part, weathered and tired, shifted about in their pews. The children stared blankly at the rotating fans, as if they were portals to another, cooler, dimension. "I said that the Lord said, 'I go to prepare a place for you'!"

Rosehill Baptist Church was ornate. There was a line of windows along the left side of the church that opened to face a brick wall about a foot and a half away. Six metal oscillating fans were positioned throughout the church. Silk bouquets tipped off the end of every other lacquered wooden pew. The pews were not attached to the floor, and when enough children got together they usually moved them around—just to prove that they could. The deep mahogany benches were donated by the local high school's woodshop class after the Reverend Snider ran into Mr. Henry, the large egg-headed woodshop instructor with fast-blinking eyes, coming from the less-than-reputable establishment known as the Furry Cat.

The only elaborate section of the modest church would be the chancel. Large slats of marble were laid atop the wood floor, creating worlds of distance from the rest of the church. The altar was made of shining limestone and was covered with thick silken cloth. Hanging from the ceiling behind the altar was a large cross cut of the same deep red wood as the pews. The choir rested slightly off to the left in padded folding chairs. To the right was an exquisitely crafted lectern of pale birch from which the clergy would deliver the sermons.

The Reverend Snider's histrionics were off the meter, but despite their sticky discomfort, the parishioners began to respond with a broken chorus of "Amen's," "Yes sir's," and "Umm-hmm's."

"Now, church," he continued, "I didn't say the Lord said— Hold on a second now, can you hear me, church?" He backed a few steps from the pulpit for dramatic effect, Jheri curls whipping about like a crown of irate eels, hands and arms flapping like a launching eagle. "I didn't say 'in a little while,' did I?"

A rousing round of "No's" came from the congregation, which was either (1) catching the Holy

Ghost, or (2) catching on to the fact that the Reverend Snider was not going to let them go until they joined in his fervor. They had been here before, when the Reverend's zealous, unwavering devotion to the Lord and all-consuming faith became their own.

"Deacon Brown," said the minister, turning to a thin man seated on his side of the altar, "did the Lord say, 'In a little while'?"

"No, sir," the deacon replied, shook his head, smiled, snapped his fingers, tapped his foot.

Heads swayed, shoulders jostled, spirits lifted. One woman began rocking back and forth. A man stood up and let out a hearty "Preach, Reverend. Preach." The Holy Spirit must have been a jack rabbit that day, because the passion broke out in disparate corners—two in the front, three in the back, one on that side, two on the other. Within moments, there was not a man, woman, or child in the church who was not hypnotized by the preacher's sermon.

Save two.

"I'ma make a place for myself," Michael grinned, turning to Diamond.

Deacon Brown got up and handed out two silver collection plates on either side of the church.

"I said—listen now, brothers and sisters," — waving his unfolded cloth through the air. "I said, the Lord said, 'I *go*'! Meaning *right now*, brothers and sisters. *Not* tomorrow . . . *Not*, after I finish making the payments on my shiny new car . . . *Not*, once little Timothy's college education is secured . . ."

Diamond rolled his eyes. *Who in here could afford a new car?* His mom was out working overtime just so he didn't have to step into the Lord's house with the same worn-out shoes anymore.

Men, women, and children were bright eyed under the reverend's spell. They stood and swayed like weak trees in a breeze, or nodded in agreement like broken slaves. The deacon shimmied back and forth in a sanctified jitterbug as Shirley led the choir through "Hail, Sweet Jesus."

Hail sweet Jesus / His love is divine / Hail sweet Jesus / His salvation is mine . . .

Michael was fixed on the shiny silver plate which was slowly filling up with loose change and paper money.

The priest continued on, about the Lord making a place for those who made a place for Him. The choir accentuated his words. The Hallelujahs and Amens went on. The fans made their turns.

The plate made its way to Diamond. He dropped in one of the two dollar bills his mother had left on the dresser that morning. Michael dropped in a single dollar, but deftly retrieved it, along with a fistful of bills, stuffing them into his pocket.

"Michael! What are you doing?" Diamond whispered harshly.

Michael's eyes were black suns with a Medusa effect. He had a veneer of permanent mean that glossed his thin lips and squashed his nose. He laughed like no nine-year-old should be able to.

The stare froze Diamond; the giggles vibrated to his marrow. Swiping pennies from heaven may not rank with eating of the forbidden tree or looking back at the burning city, but Michael's move was not totally unprecedented. He had already committed a long list of petty atrocities that only the most trustworthy of untrustworthy youths were privy to: the constant heists from Murphy's Candy Store, the pilfering of other students' bags during recess, the quick dips into purses at the butcher shop, the "free" fruit from the Korean stands. Diamond knew his friend would see that one moment—ill-hearted deed or twist of verbiage—with which he would cast his lot with the damned.

Diamond and Michael spent that summer in gluttonous abandon. Peering over the rooftop guardrails of Diamond's building, they snacked on large Macintosh apples, an assortment of candies, potato chips and snacks, quarter waters, and whatever other bounty they had procured from the day's runs. Below, children frolicked about, rode bikes, jumped rope, and played hide-and-seek in dizzying circles around the clumps of young men tumbling dice on the asphalt and blaring music.

"Why you think them dummies runnin' around?" Michael asked.

"Have fun?" Diamond spat out a shower of sunflower seed shells.

"Unh-uhh," Michael shook his head. "They runnin' from school. Like, they think if they keep runnin' and runnin' and runnin', they can keep up with summer and never have to go back to school, back to teachers, back to people telling them what to do, right and wrong."

Diamond shrugged his shoulders. They had been popping sweets for the better part of two hours, and the sugar rush was known to turn any kid into a ghetto philosopher. He remembered one Lemon Licker and Tastee Pop–induced frenzy that left the two of them pondering why they always had to keep *something* open in the winter: When the heat was on, it would be so hot that they had to pull up the windows; when it was off, an opened, heated oven was used to keep the apartment warm. They had spent all night coming up with a solution to the "open" problem, but couldn't remember it when they awoke hung over and drained the next morning.

"Me, I ain't runnin', 'cause I ain't going back to school," Michael said. "School's for suckers."

"That's the candy talking. You know you shouldn't be mixing Cheesie Sticks with Peenut Spikes, man. That's a bad combo."

"Nah, I'm serious." He sucked his teeth.

"Alright," Diamond conceded. "Then, what's your ma gonna say?"

Another suck of the teeth. Michael peered into nothingness. The question hung in the air like the discarded sneakers dangling from telephone wires all over the neighborhood. Diamond immediately realized his slip of the tongue.

Michael's mom suffered from the most prolonged case of post-partum depression ever heard of. This was not a clinical observation, mind you. It came from the real authorities, who earned their credentials courtesy of peripheral hearing through open windows, during the spin cycles in the laundry room, and in between sips of cold beer and cheap liquor in plastic cups during midafternoon sports wrap-ups on tattered couches on the corner ("Can you believe that Gooden?! Beatin' up on his wife when he got all that money and coke! Boy, I can't wait for basketball season to come back." Sip. "By the way, the Williams lady in 312 is crazy as a kook ain't she?").

One afternoon, when Michael was four years old, his mom went to the store and never came back. He waited for her return for months. It was something he couldn't understand. She had taken her keys, her list, and said she'd be right back. Michael was a bit surprised that she had left him alone in the apartment, but figured it was not that different from the long hours when she would close the door to her room, peer out the window, or gaze blankly at the TV set. He would bawl while his stomach chewed on itself, only to be placed in the closet or left on the fire escape when she returned to wakeful consciousness.

So she left him alone. It couldn't have been that big a deal. Especially the way his father came home, saw his wife of eight years gone, and quietly cooked his own dinner. Father began taking care of his son without missing a beat, without filing a police report, without making a phone call.

"I ain't got no Ma," Michael said.

Diamond's eyes and thoughts wandered to the souped-up, cherry red Volvo with tinted windows pulling into the parking lot down to the left. Out of it came Mighty Mike Cee. Children ran to him like the Son, while girls coyly made their way into his line of view.

Diamond was mesmerized by Mike's large gold cables and Gucci suit; his white Kangol hat. *That's me*, Diamond thought. *His songs are played on the radio even during the day*.

Though he had never dared bust a rap in front of anyone other than the man in the mirror, Diamond could see his future in Technicolor with Dolby sound. The magazine covers, his headlining tour, his Grammy acceptance speech: *"I'd like to thank God, for giving me life; my mother, sitting right there in the front row, for standing by my side; my best friend, Michael, for being my best friend; Michael Jackson for singing background on my first seven hits . . ."*

He would leave the projects behind, buy Ma a house in the Hamptons, a car or two, and a gold chain or maybe six, for himself, load up on stock in Jujyfruit—

"Oh shit!" Michael pointed down to a commotion a few buildings away. "Larry B's whupping Silver Slim's ass!"

Larry's real name is Laurentia Bautista, a crude reflection of the Sicilian-Dominican highball that is his parentage. He was born in Italy but spent his formulative years in the Andes of Colombia, harvesting cocoa leaves and seemingly on the run from the rest of the world. The authorities were yellow-teethed, stubble-chinned, uncleansed demons to be avoided like poisonous locusts. For undisclosed reasons, his father was hated so deeply by the Mafia that even Lauren Ciancarlo was not allowed to return to the Mediterranean; and the lowlanders routinely terrorized the intruder with the flaxen-haired *blanca* and the *negrito*. Even the communities of the other mountain dwellers shunned the alien family, occasionally chasing them up to the tundra, where they would be forced to stay for days.

The young boy was born as blue black as an unforgiving midnight, but, still, the South American sun baked him with a vengeance. It was his immortal enemy, like the desert to a wounded traveler. The ultraviolet rays beat an ancient song on his skin through the thick foliage. Soon, the tireless yellow orb became his only friend outside of his family; it was the only thing that didn't run from, or after, him.

He could not understand why he was an outcast. Surely it wasn't his skin color—though many of their faces came in the lighter shades of brick, dusk, and dawn, Laurentia was no darker than a good number of the others and he praised the same God that they did. This he knew from the times he would sneak into the lowlands and hide in the bushes as the farming collectives sat in large circles, swigging down strong brews, playing guitars, and loving life by light of fire. They would share news of hunting grounds ripe with game, grazing spots abundant with growth for their livestock, and forest remedies for every ailment known to man.

Laurentia never imagined himself part of their

world, nor did he long to be. He was curious as to their customs, and that was that. To find out their ways was all that mattered.

When his family couldn't sell their leaves, Pedro would trek down to the villages that lie in the valleys and—if they were lucky—steal slow or infirm livestock for food. At times they weren't so blessed: Pedro Bautista would be gone for days to return adorned with only animal bites and small cats under his arms or a dog slung over his shoulder.

Once, after his father was gone for an ominously long time, Laurentia snuck into town despite his mother's warnings. When he returned to their hidden shack, he explained to his mother what he had heard—how their man must have been in a fight with a rabid stray, because he was at least a day and a half with the fever when the townsfolk caught him grappling with a chicken; how the thief was caught and thrashed, dragged through the streets, violated with the handle of a plow; even how worn the wasteland where his body was said to be decomposing among animal feces and the like.

Lauren was distraught. Had she not felt the intoxicated breath of the mob on her neck, she would have had a breakdown. She knew they could not make it in the wilderness on their own and that there was little, aside from herself, that she could offer as payment for passage out of the country. Unprotected and unclaimed, how many people would she have to pay? How many times?

In how many ways? The thoughts rattled her soul more than losing her only child.

She would be allowed to beg for forgiveness at home. The family would come and get her once she was able to get word to them. But they would never accept her dark child—the family denied him and might even kill him. She told Laurentia of a fabled land of opportunity where he could build a new life. "I know you will never forget what has happened here," she said. "Though I will pray that you don't remember."

Laurentia was small, yet strong enough to work as a hand on one of the ships that made its way to Cuba. From there he would be on his own to reach the promised land. "It is only a stone's throw away," his mother informed him with a rushed hug and a hurried benediction. It would be the last time they ever saw each other.

A lifetime later, Larry B emerged as a strong-arm hustler, becoming the most respected crime figure in Brooklyn's West Grove projects. Aided by preternatural powers of persuasion, a quick trigger finger, and bone-crushing arms, Larry was pushing all the pimps and heroin dealers out of the projects, one by one. He had a seemingly end-less supply of small white pebbles that he referred to as his "magic rocks." And they must have been magic, because everyone who tried them would see things no one else could see and would claim abilities of flight.

Silver Slim was a homegrown pimp who prac-ticed a different form of magic. He pumped his whores full of Pink Champale, hermetic witticisms, and slick words. Larry's magic rocks upset Slim. They broke his spells; made his women scattered and forgetful. Still, Slim was a master of the occult, and he weaved his own enchantments to counter the effects of Larry's magic rocks. It was only a matter of time before the sorcerers faced off in battle.

Even from fourteen stories above, the beating seemed brutal.

SMAKK! Whapp! PAP!

Larry's huge arms unleashed a fast and unholy havoc, planting Slim square on his ass.

SLAP! A quick backhand across the grill sent the pimp back-pedaling on his palms and heels.

THOKK! Slim's head bounced off the ground.

Slim reached into the pocket of his silk pants, pulled out a six-inch stiletto, and dug it squarely into Larry's kneecap.

Larry grinded his good leg into Slim's ribs with a crackling effect.

The battle was over by the time Michael and Diamond reached downstairs.

Slim's blood dotted the concrete. Larry marked his passing with a crimson line of his own that went around the building.

Neighbors gathered and recounted the tale: "He musta flew twenny feet!" . . . "Man, I bet they heard his jaw crack all the way in Katmandu!"

Tamara rode circles with her pink Schwinn. She stopped and called to Diamond, who came running.

"You not gonna go over there are you?" she asked.

"Well . . . I was just . . . who me? No, I was with Michael and he said he had to, umm . . . I mean, we were just walking by and—"

"I don't like Michael. He's ugly and he steals. You don't steal with him, do you Diamond?"

"Me? Steal?" He paused. "I don't steal. I don't know nothing about no stealing. We were just going to see, uhh, Miss Mallory, to see if she needed anything done with her cats, because I wanted to see if we—"

"That's good, Diamond. Don't steal. Stealing's bad. I made a dress for my dolly. Wanna see?" She pulled out a rag doll that was wrapped up in what seemed to be a piece of an old tablecloth.

Michael followed Larry's trail around the building like a bloodhound.

"I should work for you, Mr. B," he said, catching up to the limping man.

"Get out of my face." Larry applied pressure right above his wounded knee before sliding himself down the wall to sit on the ground.

"Listen, Mr. B, you big an' strong an' all, but that hole in your leg is gonna have you out of commission for a few days. I figure I can watch things for you until you get back on your feet."

Larry was sweating profusely and breathing heavily. "What can you do for me, Slick? You ain't nuttin' but a tapeworm in the belly of this beast. Beat it."

"I can sell for you in front of 404, and, unlike

Sando, who you got there now, I won't smoke none o' your magic rocks."

Larry let go of his leg and blood shot up like a small geyser. He reached into his pocket, pulled out and gave Michael a .22 semiautomatic handgun. "Go and tell that motherfucker he's out of business. If you're working 404 when I get back, we'll talk." He stood up and wambled away, leaning onto the building.

There are different versions as to how Michael removed Sando from the front of building number 404. Some say he shot the old dealer right in his heart and killed him. But, knowing that even a crackhead could survive a .22 slug, that story holds no weight. Besides, to this day Sando is known to be around Red Hook projects begging for spare change to support his drug habit. Still, there are those who say that it is really not Sando in Red Hook, but just some miscellaneous junkie, because Sando either: (1) went to rehab and moved to Boston where he works as a security guard; (2) was run over by a sanitation truck plowing snow during the dreadful winter of '94; or (3) thought he could fly and one day took a step over one of the buildings' guardrails, kissing the ground as a mix of crushed bone and liquefied tissue.

But what transpired is not important. What is important is that when nightfall came, Michael was in front of that building, an apprentice pushing magic rocks.

That is, until Lucie, his stepmother, got wind of

his activities. His father was working a double at the factory where he stitched MADE IN U.S.A. tags on imported wears and wouldn't be home until after midnight. It was Lucie's moral obligation to save her beloved's only son from a dead-end existence. Out she came in her waitress uniform, bustling to building 404, ordering Michael into the house.

Michael was giving a customer a small plastic-wrapped bundle of enchantment. He sucked his teeth, dissed and dismissed her with a glib comment about her "barren womb."

Lucie reeled back and smacked Michael so hard that his nose bled after he slammed to the ground. It wasn't the first time she had hit him, but she had never been so righteous in her anger. Not only was he selling crack, but she was shocked at the boy's revelation. No one, not even his father (*especially not his father!*) knew about her condition.

Michael wasn't sure how he knew what he knew. All that mattered at the time was that the bitch slapped him. Did she not know that he now had purpose? Responsibility? Escape?

Not to mention the .22 burning itself into his palm.

The gun's power was alluring. It was only a bit heavier than the cap guns he would chase Diamond through the train yards with, but this one brought a small jolt of pain along with its burst of smoke. He was drunk off its authority.

Michael got to his feet, raised the tiny handgun

to his father's second wife's face, and squeezed off two shots.

The first entered underneath her jaw and exited through the right side of her mouth, the second pierced right below her right eye and lodged near the base of her skull.

She fell back, leaving a cascading arch of blood that seemed to hang in the air forever before meeting the ground.

Lucie would never eat solid food again; she would never walk without assistance; without the aid of sunglasses, she would never be able to go out during the day. And even then, her vision would be compromised by amoeba-like blue spots.

Michael was sent upstate to a juvenile detention center for eighteen months. "Hopefully, you'll learn something you can use for life," the wrinkled white man behind the bench said. "Due to your own family's unwillingness to testify on your behalf during these proceedings, you will be turned over as a ward of the State upon your release." With a slam of the judge's gavel, two large guards escorted Michael behind big steel doors.

As promised, a year and a half later, Michael Williams was sent to a foster home run by an elderly couple. His second night there, he snuck out through a window and made his way back to the hood.

DIRTY CASH

In a corner pocket of an avoided section of the wrong part of an ignored town is Tiny's Social Emporium, a hole in the wall. It's a hole in the wall in the best sense, though—hidden, minimal, and functional. "Emporium" may be a bit hyperbolic, but, depending on what you're looking for, Tiny's can present a cornucopia of stimulation, gratification, and elation.

The spot offers no more in accommodations than a one-shelf bar, small round tables, a TV, and three pool tables. All the other entertainment walks through the door or comes from the back "office."

The manager was totalling the night's receipts when he was interrupted.

"I'm here to see Mr. B," the boy stated.

"Don't you belong at home?"

"I am home."

Larry, Crusher, and JT sat around the small desk in the back room.

"That's another hundred," JT said, tossing a pile of singles into the middle of the desk. He yawned, leaned back, and rubbed his face. "We need to expand, Larry. We can't keep running this whole thing by ourselves. We're taking too many risks."

"Patience," Larry said. "We can't grow too quickly."

"JT's right," Crusher said. "TNT was out there today."

"Yeah, those narcs don't play by the rules. They jump out those vans with their guns blazing like this is the Wild West or something."

"We'll be alright."

"That's easy for you to say, Larry. You're never out there like we are. It's getting not to be worth it." JT tipped his baseball cap back. He was way too young to have a receding hairline.

"How are the kids holding up?"

"They're cool," Crusher replied. "But they're beginning to get greedy. They think we're making more than we are."

"How's the one you put in the hospital yesterday?"

"He should be getting out tomorrow. Couple a' fractured ribs, broken collar bone, dislocated jaw, a li'l concussion."

"Christ," said JT, looking at Crusher's sculptured body. "He's only sixteen."

"He disrespected me on the ave."

"Crusher's right. We can't afford to have any revolutionaries—all a movement needs is a leader. But when that kid gets back on the strip in the morning with a new attitude, they'll all take heed." Larry grabbed his cane, its worn wood dug splinters into his hand. "Where's Tin?"

"Don't know."

"Did he call in?" Larry asked.

"Nah," said JT. "You think the cops got him?"

"Tin's a jellyfish." Larry laughed. "If he'd gotten caught, we'd all be in the station house right now."

There was a knock at the door. The manager came in, irate and red.

"Larry, I don't know what the fuck you guys are doing, but now you have kids coming through my fuckin' place."

Larry raised one eyebrow.

"Some kid is out there asking for a Mr. B. He won't leave."

" 'Mr. B'?" JT and Crusher laughed.

"Ahh," Larry said, leaning satisfied in his chair behind the desk. "The prodigal son has returned."

It was the morning of Diamond's sixteenth birthday. Michael guided him through Tiny's with a bottle of champagne in each hand. They walked past pool-playing toughs and women who all but had prices tattooed across their exposed breasts. One man put down his pool cue and waved Michael over.

"You know those new Air Jordans, the blue ones?" he asked, pulling out a knot of twenties from his pocket. He gave Michael six of the bills. "Ten and a half," he said.

"A-ight," Michael said. "Soon as I get back from talking to Mr. B."

"Don't take all day, now," the man said in a way that suggested that Michael was prone to taking his sweet time.

"C'mon, Diamond." Michael ushered his friend to a back door marked PRIVATE.

When the boys burst into the office, Mr. B was sitting cross-legged behind the desk, his cane at his side. It was a deep wood that had been polished black with a gold cobra on its head. He was decked out in a spotless white suit that seemed to flow off his body like water over smooth pebbles.

Crusher was behind wearing a plain tank top that cried for mercy from stretching around his huge pecs. On his upper left arm was a tattoo of a man holding a broken spine in his hands, which bulged every time he curled his dumbbell.

"My nigga's sixteen!" Michael shouted.

"Well, congratulations." Mr. B smiled at Diamond and shook his hand with long slender fingers. The altercation with Slim had left Mr. B with one good leg, but his grip was still as strong as a lock-jawed pitbull.

"What can I do for you?" he asked.

"You know my boy raps, right, Mr. B?"

"Is that so?" He looked Diamond up and down. "You any good?"

"Any good? This nigga's the best, the best, the best," Michael said.

Mr. B smiled approvingly.

"I was wondering if you could introduce him to some of your friends, y'know?"

"What is a friend, Gage?" Mr. B asked.

Diamond shuddered. He had heard Michael's

26

street name before, but never in conversation; it was always Michael referring to himself in the third person—"That nigga Gage this" or "Let me tell you something about this nigga Gage . . ." To hear the name fall off the tongue of the neighborhood's most notorious gangster concretized much for him in that small room. Perhaps, too much.

"Mr. B, I just wanted to know if you could help him out with his career. Diamond's good peoples."

There was a flicker in Mr. B's eyes and silence in the room. The eyes meant he had come up with an idea. The silence meant that he would keep it to himself until the time was right. Mr. B had the patience of a crocodile waiting for her young to hatch.

"Gage, what do I know about the music business?" Mr. B asked facetiously. "I'm a real-estate broker."

Crusher laughed. And not just because he was on Mr.B's payroll.

"Let me tell you something, Diamond," the businessman continued. "This world is a fucked-up place. Even this country, this land of opportunity, where money floats around like turds in a cesspool, it's hard to make a living. Very hard.

"But there are three people who must always get paid by every decent human being who makes contributions to this society, this world: that's the doctor—when you come into this place; the landlord—when you stay in this place; and the undertaker—when you leave this place.

"Now," the man continued, sounding like a

gangster again, "I ain't one for seeing a whole lot of pussy that I can't have, so being a doctor is out. And death is something I deal with only when I have to. I believe the company you keep is who you become—if you hang around with enough dead people, you'll wake up and find yourself like Jimi Hendrix."

Crusher gave an appreciative nod at his boss's turn of phrasing.

"You see me, I like to be the landlord. I buy my buildings, like this fine establishment you're in now, set up a super, and collect my money on the eighteenth of each and every month."

Mr. B stole a glance at Gage but stayed focused on the young man in front of him. There was something about Diamond that spoke to him—a sense of character, ethic, resolve. No, Diamond was not tough-guy material—far from it. His optical pieces were too soft and perfect—not wide apart like a leader, disciplined assassin, or master liar; or bunched together like a follower, unbridled killer, or one who conceals the truth without telling lies. His face was smooth and relaxed, not marked from tension or anger. His skin was a flawless butterscotch, which made him look pretty, for lack of a better description. But his stride, his demeanor, his stance—the way his feet rooted firmly to the ground—made him his own man. Diamond would stab the eyes of the sun for love and honor, but never under order.

Only sixteen, eh? Mr. B was thoroughly impressed. Diamond was one to keep at your side, never under you, where you would stifle his growth. And never, ever behind you, where he could pierce your lungs the first time you crossed him.

Gage saw all this, if only on a less articulate level. It was the reason he and Diamond had been friends all these many years. It was the reason they prearranged the marriage of their firstborn offspring. Diamond had all that Gage lacked, and vice versa. Diamond would do what should be done, must be done. Gage would do everything else.

Of what he gleaned in that Instamatic flicker and moment of silence, the above is what Mr. B would share with Crusher and the rest of his men in the coming years. The rest of his knowledge would be kept in his mental library and given out on a need-to-know basis.

"Crusher, get some glasses for this champagne," Mr. B ordered. "We have a birthday to celebrate."

The convertible grabbed the mountain's bend, its tires screaming a rebellious antiphon across the road. They were going too fast, took the turn too wide. The car crossed onto the opposite lane and missed the railing by the width of a dime.

"Mike!" Diamond yelled. "You're supposed to slow down around corners."

The road took a vicious turn in the opposite direction. The engine roared as the ride shifted gears and bit into the tar.

"Don't be such a pussy," the driver laughed. "And I told you, it's 'Gage,' alright?"

"My bust—that's gonna take a second to get used to."

"Make it a fast one."

They came to a straightaway and Michael's foot was dead weight on the gas pedal. The trees and water were an aquamarine slideshow with a hurricane soundtrack whipping in their ears. The car dipped in and out of traffic like a coked-up bumble bee.

Diamond dug his hands into the dashboard. "Slow down!"

"Okay, okay," Michael laughed, shifting down. "Don't want to kill you on your birthday and all."

The car coasted along the highway.

"Nigga, we livin'!" Michael screamed to the world. He turned to Diamond. "C'mon, kid, we sixteen, we got a ride, money in our pocket—what else is there?"

Michael had been repeating their age all day as if it gave them entrance to a secret dominion where being sixteen meant that everything was alright. Diamond wasn't sure how Michael was making his money, but he knew it had to do with those afternoons in Tiny's Emporium, running errands for Mr. B. The few who dared invoke the gangster's name in the hood spoke with reverence or under anonymity. Yet Gage was casual friends with the man. And Diamond was best friends with Michael. It was unnerving, but natural.

"You hear what happened to Malik?" Diamond asked.

"Your cousin?"

"Yeah. Nobody could fuck with Malik on the

court. He has an outside jumper that can't miss. You know the nigga made starting All City three years in a row. Coaches, press, talent scouts, everyone says he's heading straight for the NBA. But this kid who balled for Eastern was shot in the back four times by police. They said he was pulling 'something shiny' out of his gym bag—"

"I heard about that."

"So," Diamond continued, "Malik's team made a decision to wear all of their jerseys backwards—they were going to do it until the case was solved, on some real protest shit. The referees played along for a few games, then they said it was against regulations. No, it wasn't implicitly denied in the rules, but neither was hanging from the rim with your hand on your crotch after a dunk, and they made those damned jungle bunnies stop doing that, didn't they? Ingrates. Wouldn't have them running around like the gym is a freakin' zoo and they think they can start some damned civil rights movement? Maybe on some other hardwood floors, but not in White E. Ford High.

"Anyway, the refs would not allow anyone to play unless they wore their jerseys like the great white basketball gods intended. Malik wasn't having it. After he missed three games, coach threw him offa the team."

"Word? That's fucked up," Michael said. "I keep telling you man: Organized sports is no place to be a man."

They made their way into the city and pulled up in front of Manhattan's Grand Central Station amid horns, cabs, buses, and pedestrians.

"Yo, take this joint home," Michael said, stepping out of the car. "Rush-hour traffic is gonna kill you."

"What?"

"Go see Tamara or something. You done been chasing her down since we was little. Maybe she'll see you in this and give you some."

"You know she ain't like that."

"Nigga you sixteen, now. You can't be running around virginized much longer."

"I ain't no virgin."

"Whatever."

Michael disappeared into the sea of people entering the station. They bustled through the great caverns, glancing at timepieces with hollow eyes, briefcases lugged at arm's length.

He boarded the New Haven train with a wave of bobbing commuters. The iron beast hissed, chugged, jolted, moved out. It was worming its way through the city's concrete bowels when a scuffle erupted midcar.

Crusher pulled a large man by his lapels and pushed the wind out of him with an angry knee to the diaphragm. The man's face turned red with horror as he collapsed and writhed on the floor, barely strong enough to curl up like a fetus.

Crusher pulled the quaking man to his feet and rammed him against the train doors repeatedly before flinging his limp body into the aisle.

JT emerged from the far corner of the train with a sawed-off Browning 12-gauge resting in his shoulder.

Mr. B folded his newspaper, placed it in his

armpit, and stood from his seat. "Now," he began, carefully manuevering his cane around the unconscious man. "We have a Great Train Robbery planned for today. There are many ways this can happen. One of them is lying here on the floor. Another is my co-worker here." JT pumped the shotgun. "But that's not all. More surprises await you. Tin?"

Tin got up from his seat and slapped together a Kalashnikov AK-47 from a cello case.

"But there is another way this can go. Gage?" Michael pulled out a burlap sack the size of Kris Kringle's and began rustling the passengers for their valuables. "The choice is yours," Mr B said.

"This is a test." He caned up and down the car like a dignitary addressing grave social issues. "This is only a test. If this were an actual hijacking, you would all be on a plane taking us to a country with no extradition treaties."

Diamond had driven down blocks of mansions with manicured lawns and spaced driveways before stopping at the two story with large windows and an apple tree out front. The red fruit hung lightly and were so perfect they could have been photographed for a brochure. The lawn was a radiant emerald with a KEEP OFF THE GRASS sign separated by a gravel walkway that led to a flag patio.

He stood at the door of the corbie gable.

"That *is* what my mother named me," he told the woman.

"Well, I have to see if Tamara's home," she said with a slam of the door and a twist of the bolt.

He was still waiting. He would have waited forever. When she finally came down, her hair was still wet and she smelled like flowers and soap.

"Diamond. What are you doing here?" Tamara asked.

"I was in the neighborhood, so . . ."

"You? In this neighborhood?" An old white man wearing plaid shorts and flip-flops walked by with a pedicured collie. "Yeah, okay," she laughed.

"I take it your mom doesn't care for me. Seems like she's changed since she left the projects, like she doesn't know who's who or what's what."

"We're not like that," Tamara said. "Hold on, I made you something for your birthday."

She came back to the door with a gun holster made from a rawhide purse and a cowboy belt. He could wear it around his waist with the gun on either hip, in the small of his back, or in his pelvic region, without its ever being detected. "I don't know, I just made it and it reminded me of you. Or I was thinking of you and it came out that way. I'm not sure which."

"You need to go into business with this stuff," Diamond said, rubbing his hands over the stitching. "You been doing it since I've known you."

"Please," she protested. "I'd like to go to a fashion college or something. But I'm being realistic. I'm going to a real school, getting my real degree, and getting me a real job. What about you? You know you better start thinking about college."

"You always thinking practical and all that,"

Diamond said sheepishly, eyeing the plush lawn. "I guess school'll come around when it comes around." He paused. "I roasted nine guys in a rhyme cipher last week. Can't nobody out here rhyme better than me."

"All that's good, Diamond. But don't you want to do something with your life?"

"That *is* what I wanna do with my life."

"I mean to make money, support yourself."

He didn't have an answer for her. He couldn't see himself working day in and day out, just to come home, sleep, and do the same thing again the next day. Diamond was not the type to live for the weekends. Tamara would never understand that for him it was the big stage or bust. There was no plan B.

"Wanna go for a ride?" he asked, motioning to the convertible.

"Diamond!" She was shocked. "What did you do to get that car?"

"It's not mine. It's Ga— Michael's."

She looked at Diamond and his birthday present. It seemed like an omen and she knew why she had made it for him. Her heart throbbed and bunched up in her throat.

Something in her eyes begged him not to ever need it, but it was hidden, covered by the part of her that left the projects behind. She would never love a soldier, policeman, or a nigga from the hood—no one you'd receive a middle-of-the-night visit about.

Her eyes welled up. "I have to go," she said.

BLUE ANGEL

With the exception of its citrus complexion, East New York's West Grove Housing Complex is much like any other—a sprawling eyesore of brick, glass, and despair rising from its dilapidated surroundings, as much a marriage of form and function as any jail or necropolis can be.

Garbage perfumes the area with a rancidity that most residents have long grown immune to. Pigtailed young girls jump double Dutch on uneven sidewalks. The police roll through, three-deep in mobile houses of pain, passing off feigned concern and lazy friendship, giving the area a sense of occupied territory. In the morning, workers make an exodus to their blue-collar positions, and in the evening return, tired and frustrated, cursing their existence. The old men talk sports ("I can't believe they took Gooden back . . .") sitting on dirty lawn chairs underneath torn beach umbrellas.

The apartment of Rose and Diamond St. James would send an interior decorator into conniptions. In the living room, the couch and love seat appear to be distant cousins; the television set lacks knobs and an antenna (though pliers and a hanger provide); the bookshelf, two shades removed from any other wooden object in the home, is full of worn tomes that have not been opened this decade. The battle-scarred kitchen table wobbles like a drunk, even though a short stack of magazines is propped underneath one leg. The refrigerator, stove, and cabinets are archaic models whose joints squeak with the slightest movement. The floor tiles were once white but have since acquired a permanent film of dirt that gives them a dull, grayish tint in the dim lights.

The walls in the kitchen, like the bathroom, show age-old cement where whole large portions of tile have fallen off. Every water opening in the apartment leaks, giving a light smell of must and dampness.

Throughout the apartment, winged cockroaches move about with the casualness of a Welfare inspector, rummaging through garbage, closets, and the fridge all the same.

And then there's Diamond's room.

The sounds coming in through my window—the laughing kids, police sirens, caterwauling winos, and filaments of gossip (something about some nigga not knowing who she was, how many other men she could have, how she didn't need his shit when she already got two kids to take care of . . .)—wake me up. They wake me up every morning. I lie in bed for a minute, listening to hungry rats scurry through the walls, tuning into the knocking, bubbling, and gurgling of the pipes, finding out (again) what the lady upstairs gets when she stays out too late. It takes a while for me to sit up.

When I do, the room spins and my head thumps like I have one-thousand-watt Cerwin-Vega subwoofers attached to my temples. The half-empty liquor bottles on the window sill remind me why. I give up on focusing—involuntary vertigo is so much more comforting than the seaship sway of trying to keep your thoughts straight during the morning after.

There's a funny dance going on as I round the bed, looking for the condom. My legs don't quite buckle as they never fully get straight—just an accordion-like expansion and contraction that accompanies my mating groove. My hands are responding to my thoughts slower than the superintendent to a maintenance request. Just as well; figure I'd miss it if I go too fast anyway.

Where is it? Coulda swore I left it around here somewhere . . .

I sift through the magazines spread across the floor, fumble through a pile of tees and undies in the corner—not there. Search through the folds of my blanket—not there either. Toss the blanket aside—it's gotta be in the sheets.

Nothing.

Gotta clear my head. The room is spinning again. I need to take a leak.

As I piss, head resting on the wall, I feel the coolness of the bathroom tiles under my feet, on my temples. It almost makes things better, wakes me up, centers me.

Almost.

Back to the room.

Damned. It reeks of sweat, pussy, and booze.

Where's that Jim hat?

I pick up the blanket and flap it across the bed. The used rubber flies across the room like a trapeze artist and lands on my keyboard.

I try to remember her name as I wrap it up in a tissue.

Met her in the Palace, so it may have been Alice, the way she played with my phallus, tossed salads, and marked my back with her talons. All the same, she may have been Sharane. Devoid of game, her approach was lame. Damned . . . what *was* her name?

I did meet her at the Palace, of that I'm sure. Michael had left with some red-bone chick, fine as crystal. Nigga's always going for them light-skin honeys; nothing but gold and platinum. I just pray he doesn't come back with a white girl one day. Don't think I could take it.

Damned. What *was* Shorty's name?

"I wanna do something," she had said. Her skin was soft, her smile fragile, her gaze was set on my reputation, not me. "Let's go out, go get something to eat."

It was 2 A.M. "Love, we in the 'hood. The only thing you can get at this time is weed, liquor, chips, and gas."

"Let's get some gas. Lots of gas." She stretched

her arms like that batty white chick in *Breakfast at Tiffany's*. "I want to go around the world."

So, I gassed her alright. Came back with fifths of vodka, Schnapps, cognac, and scotch. Cracked the vodka, told her we'd start our worldwide jaunt in Russia. She didn't get it and downed the shots like an amateur—one right after the other, not giving them time to settle in.

Five minutes later, she was hot as a muskrat in July.

I sipped lightly, remembering what Shakespeare said about the spirits' ability to give the desire but rob the ability.

Still can't remember her name though. Hope she got home okay. She *was* a sleeping drunk when I put her in the back of that cab.

It's hot this morning. Too hot for September. Must be one of those Indian summers or El Niño or something. I go to the bathroom, wash my face, head back to my room, and fire up the equipment. The amp gives off its low-level hum, the tape deck whirls awake. I pop in the track from last week and the sound explodes. I write.

Leave your body on the ground with chalk around it / Just to show you that I'm 'bout it, 'bout it / Diamond St. / The one you doubted / So, you could sip on Dom P all you want, G / You still couldn't harm me / African killer bees couldn't swarm me / I'll read your card like a Swami / Bring your bass to your ass like Miami / With my own army / West Grove / These projects'll bring it to any set / Demoting generals to cadets / With shorties that'll kill you over wack sex /

Pulling chrome nines out of Avirex jackets / I burn like the sun / Your glow runs short like matches . . .

The pages fill with lines, stanzas, tangents, and yes, the perfect ending to that joint from last week. After about three pages, the phone rings.

I ignore it.

A few moments later, Ma cracks the door. "Tamara's on the phone."

"Yo."

"Yo?" she questions. "Anyway . . . You stood me up last night, because . . ."

"I'm sorry, I was in the studio. Real last minute."

"And you were struck with convenient amnesia, couldn't remember my number, then Fidel Castro needed you to write a rhyme for his new album, so you had to fly to Cuba? . . . Whatever, Diamond. Am I your girl or what? Why you don't want to see me? Do you even care—"

"Slow down. Don't put it on me like that. I'm juggling a lot and sometimes—"

"Oh, I have to be juggled in now?"

Tamara's a smart chick. I really like her. But ever since we started going out about a year ago, she's turned real stupid. Clingy. Demanding. Crying. Like she's watched one too many episodes of *My So-Called Life*. I never knew why MTV was the scourge of the planet until she started watching that show and got all Angela on me.

"Why the grief this early in the morning?" I ask.

"Why you gotta leave me wondering if you're dead or alive? You're always keeping me in the dark. That's not how you treat someone you say you love . . ."

I lean back and rest on the refrigerator. We're out of bread and running low on cereal. Hey, what's Ma doing home from work so early? I rub my hand across my face and over my head. The frazzled ends remind me that I need to get my hair braided.

"And—you're not even listening are you?"

"Listen," I say. "I'ma come by today. I need to get my hair done."

"Yeah, can always count on that. Whenever Diamond needs his hair done, you know he'll come around."

I don't have the energy this morning. I never have the energy, but this morning I'm finding no amusement in her insecurities. Women: Can't live wit' 'em, and there's not an island big enough to fit them all on.

"Yeah, well make sure that it's early," she says. "I have a three-thirty class."

I hang up before there's room for more debate. Tamara's been around since forever. Do I love her? Yeah, whatever. I guess. Am I ready to settle down? Far from it. I'm only twenty. Give me a break.

Ma's on the couch, watching a morning news show and humming a Mary J. Blige tune.

"Whatchu know about Mary?"

"What do you know about Mary?" She's always correcting me.

"They sent me home early," she says before I can ask. That's the third time this week. She doesn't make much on her fourteen-hour shifts as a dispatcher for a local cab service, and three days' pay is a serious chunk of change to do without. I've seen her go to work with more determination than a postman through flus, colds, and all sorts of illness, so I know something must be wrong.

"Are you okay?"

"Boy, I'm fine. Don't you worry about me. I'm just having hot flashes."

"I don't need to hear all that."

"Yes you do." She laughs weakly out of the corner of her eye. "And why do you have girls leaving out of here at all times of night? You keep messing with all these little chicken legs and you'll see where it gets you."

"Heads, Ma. Chicken *heads*."

"Whatever, boy. You just make sure that you're wearing your raincoat when things get wet. I can't stop you from doing the wrong things, but I'll be damned if you're going to do the stupid things. Remember: It's easier to run up in them than it is to run out on them."

I fidget, suck a long breath, change the subject.

"So, what did the doctors really say. You've been feeling sick for a minute, now, haven't you?"

"Only a week or two." That means at least three months. "They said I'm fine. It took them all of twenty minutes to find out. You know HIP."

"Did you think about seeing another doctor? I mean a real one?"

"As a matter of fact, I did. I saw one and he said that I would be fine as soon as my son stopped asking me a million questions." She laughs weakly

43

again. "Diamond, I'm fine. It's just one of those recurring migraines or something. I'm okay once I get some aspirin in my system."

"Maybe you should kick back, take some time off. I can take care of the bills and stuff."

"Boy, what can you take care of? I haven't seen you go out for a job in months."

"C'mon, jobs come to me." I smile.

She doesn't.

"Dance like nobody's watching, sing like nobody's listening, love like you've never been hurt before, and live like there's no tomorrow," she says.

I know what that means.

"Cut the acting, boy." She leans forward, rests her hands on my knee, looks at me softly. "Diamond, I'd much rather you come back home dejected from a million job interviews than get in any deeper than you already are with Mr. Larry, Michael, and the rest of them."

Ma pauses. "You're just going to have to learn things on your own, in your own way."

The plastic slipcovers squeak when she leans back. She stares at the television, clutching the gold crucifix that always hangs around her neck. She's only eighteen years older than me, but life is seriously taking its toll on her. Her eyes glow less these days and she moves about with no direction. I see her, when she thinks I'm not looking, falling out into the bed, couch, or a chair, her head hanging low.

Ma hasn't always been like this. I remember just two summers ago, when she finally learned to ride a bike. Every Saturday morning, bright and early, she'd wake and drag me out of bed for a round through the park. It seems like a whole lifetime ago. Rocking sweats and no makeup with her hair pulled back, she could pass for my paramour. I remember, one time, I actually had to punch out some hobo who asked me how I "bagged that older bitch."

"She pro'bly married," he said, smiling through a missing tooth. "You know that's when they get at they sexual peak, start wantin' some young blood. Man, what I'd give to be eighteen again. But with my knowledge, now—heh-heh."

Ma was bent over tying her sneaker lace.

The vagrant rubbed his scraggly beard. "Man, I'd take that bitch and—"

WHAP!

I doubled the space between his teeth with a quick right jab.

"Get your mother some aspirin, boy," Ma says.

The tap water is still settling when I return.

"Don't worry, Ma. I've been putting together some tight tracks and I'm real close to finishing my demo. You just get your vocal chords in order—I'ma need someone to blaze my first radio hit with some soulful crooning."

I know that as long as she's singing, she's fighting.

She smiles at me and absent-mindedly rubs the back of my neck. Even her hand feels warm.

"I already chased one man out of my life by not allowing him to follow his dream. I won't do it to another."

I'm caught offguard by her directness. Ma hardly talks about my father, let alone so personally. And I don't like her blaming herself for his leaving. He had a choice between living his life and chasing his dream. All I can remember is him leaning over the piano with a glass of the wild juice every now and then.

I look at her hand. She still wears the wedding band; she's never gotten a divorce. It's an inexpensive show of affection, looks like it came out of a Cracker Jack box; a twirled raise of three stones—white, red, and green—that looks like a bent stoplight. I figure that she fancies herself a married woman whose husband has gone on an extended business trip. Like one day, he'll walk through the door, "Hi honey, sorry I'm late. I brought you some flowers."

She'd probably run and hug him, get his slippers, and fix his plate while he read the sports section.

But I know what I'd do if Clifford St. James ever came through the door of apartment 6S.

"My father made his own decision," I say.

The morning weatherman says there's no relief in sight. Just heat, heat, and more heat.

"Just as well." She lies back and closes her eyes.

I carefully remove her shoes, prop her head with a pillow, and kiss her on the forehead.

LOWRIDER

It's well after two o'clock by the time I shower and make my way out of the apartment.

Fuck, the elevator's not working.

I'm still cussing five flights of steps later, when I round the bend to the lobby. A shady-looking character wearing a heavy jacket darts from the landing.

I feel my wood-grained Colt Mustang .380 auto against the small of my back, in Tamara's holster, protected and protecting. My breath, heart rate, and eyes jump real quick then slow down to deep predator state. The sounds of construction outside become distinct. Every crack on the lavender walls gains high personality. Someone's frying fish. They're using a lot of pepper.

I come to the ground with my arm swinging loose, ready to grasp, pull, and squeeze if necessary.

I see Ronnie fiddling about the vestibule. "Oh," he says with a guilty smile. "It's just Diamond."

Ronnie flutters back to the steps. He doesn't

walk as much as he bounces—like cares, worries, and obligations are something that he's learned to leave for others to deal with. He's a bit taller than me, maybe about six feet, but his poking dreds and laissez-faire attitude make him appear much higher.

Steve emerges like a shadow from a hidden recess. "W'sup, D?"

"What y'all up to now?" I ask.

Steve answers with movement. He pulls a small piece of metal, inserts it into one of the mailboxes, pops it open, shuffles through the envelopes, and slides one into his back pocket. He's methodical and meticulous, like an expert craftsman. His T-shirt and jeans are crisp with starch, his sneakers brand new, white and irridescent. Only his arms move when he jerks a slot open.

After a few moments he's satisfied and whistles to Ronnie.

We walk out the building together. The sun is blinding, bouncing off the bright orange projects, basking us in the glow one would expect in a mirror-lined furnace. Pure orange.

Only West Grove projects are orange. Every other project around here is that dirty brownish red. Even the Pink Houses (named after L. H. Pink, not, obviously, the color). Not us, though. Orange.

We go around the parking lot to my Cutlass Supreme. She's gold in some parts, brown in others, with a blue hood and rusted sheen. The trunk is tied up with a piece of cord, but you can't tell that unless you give her a close inspection. Some smart-ass fingered WASH ME through the coat of dust on her window.

"Yo, man," Ronnie laughs. "We could take this bitch and— " He places his hand on the roof to settle himself from giggling. "Take this shit and torch it for insurance." He doubles over. "That's if you had any insurance!"

She had been sitting behind the basketball courts for days when I first saw her. The courts were on the far side of the projects, nearer to the factories. I imagine that, at some point, they were inspirational squares full of smiles and aspirations, but now they were just cages of shit-talking and escapist dreams. I never really went to the basketball courts, 'cause there was nothing there for me. There was no one rhyming back there and most of the girls that hung out back there were already pushing strollers or were only interested in the lanky jocks they saw as a ticket aboard the mythical chariot known as the American Dream.

The courts would have been a haven for the druggists and druggies if not for the incessant musical echo from the air-filled pumpkins that bounced off the courts from dawn 'til the dark of night. For a while, some local dealers had set up shop in the area, happy to escape the prying eyes of the neighbors in the front.

It's not that there was what one would call a view *anywhere* in West Grove, but, if anyone holds that as truth, no one acknowledges it openly. Day and night, the windows out front look like so many picture frames, with live subjects imagining beautiful horizons and visions of slow sunsets and white clouds. But around the back there was no such pretense—just graffitied walls and the black soot rising from the factories' chimneys.

Malik dragged me back there one day after he heard that Chippie Mason had been calling his name for a battle of moves after each basket he sunk. Chippie was an older cat with shoulder-length braids with rubber bands on the ends and lackluster black skin, like an old pair of shoes that never saw polishing. He was short for a ball-player, only about five foot, ten inches, but he was quick and ruthless on the court. He wasn't as much talented as he was determined to take the ball into the basket. And sometimes that's all it took.

He was the best baller on any netless play-ground from East New York straight through Coney Island. Were he able to follow rules or keep his mouth shut, he'd no doubt have made the NBA. But he was too allured by the noncommitance of the parks. Something about streetball made it the only real sport to him.

When Chippie saw Malik, everything stopped, just like in one of those Westerns where the good guy and the bad guy meet at high noon. They walked circles around each other without saying a word. If I didn't know my cousin better, I would have sworn fisticuffs were set to erupt. Even the basketballs seemed to grow weary of the situation, rolling off into far corners.

"Who got next?" asked Malik.

All the courts cleared.

Such was the respect of the two gladiators. Combined, they had bested more opponents than this country lost men in Vietnam. They had "next" whenever they stepped onto a court. Always. For them to meet each other to duel mano-a-mano was more than enough reason to forfeit any game going.

"I got Jo-Jo," said Chippie, pointing to a tall brother whose knuckles scraped the ground when he sat.

"Blue shirt," Malik said. Taxx, the waxy-skinned kid in the blue shirt, got up and ran to Malik's side.

Moments later, a full court game of shirts versus skins was going on. But, it didn't really matter who was on who's side. It was a one-on-one competition between Malik and Chippie. Everyone else was dressing.

Chippie was a bit quicker than my cousin, but Malik was still able to keep him from driving underneath the hoop. The trash-talker drew first blood when he ran up the lane, faked to the left, spun right, and hit a blind jumper over Malik's head.

Coming down the court, Malik moved like a ballerina on skates. There was no defense against him when he carried that air-filled pumpkin to the lip of the basket and let gravity do the rest.

It ran like that for the better part of an hour, with instinct and talent being met by technique and skill at every turn.

Near the end of the game, Chippie began to grow flustered. He was not used to being played so closely or computedly, and the game was so close that it had already been extended from 50 to 65, and now to 90. Regardless of the outcome, Chippie knew he had lost. He had been boasting that streetball was far superior to the organized game. In his analysis, there was no way the game should have been close. It was tied at 80.

"Game 105," Chippie declared.

"No way, man," a tall shirtless brother said, hands on knees. "We been out here for over an hour, man."

"Yeah," Jo-Jo, said, wiping sweat off his brow with a heavy breath.

"C'mon! Don't be turnin' pussy," Chippie argued. "I don't want nothing about nothing. We gon' win this game and win it right. Right?"

Chippie looked around, but no one agreed with him. Heck, no one even knew what he was talking about. 'Cept for Chippie, everyone seemed pleased with the game's outcome. Had the game died there at 80-all, it would have been the stuff of legend; fossil fuel for the stories to grandchildren when Malik broke records in the pros. "Did I ever tell you about the time I saw Sleek Malik Pendergrast go for six hours in the park against Chippie Mason? See, Chippie was King on the concrete, but Malik was the hierarchy of the hardwood. Man game was tied at two hun'red! It was a cold, dark day, not even the birds were out . . ."

"Alright," Chippie said. "Let's take a break. I'll be back." He swaggered off the court with his hands swinging from side to side in tense rhythms.

"You and your frien' best to git outta here," a girl said.

She was sitting next to me. She had lips that could pull the red off a cherry and revealed a gold tooth when she smiled. Her sly eyes seemed to be genuinely concerned.

"That nigga gon' come back wit' a gun." Her head rolled on her neck and her large earrings knocked against each other. Around her neck was a large plate that gave her name as Sharronda.

I had no idea who she was but knew that she was telling the truth, if only so I could be in debt to her at a later date. I ground my teeth and swore that I'd never leave my gun at home again.

"Malik!" I ran to the middle of the court, feeling Sharronda's eyes on my back, sizing me up for the payback. "Let's be out."

"What?" He looked at me as if I just indecently propositioned him. "Nigga, you crazy? The score is tied. I ain't goin' nowhere."

"Look, man. You brought me back here for a reason. I know these houses like Al Sharpton know trouble, now I'm telling you it's time to go."

He put his hands on his hips and squinted in the distance to see if Chippie was coming back.

"C'mon." I grabbed him by one elbow.

"Where ya'll going?" Taxx called out from the side of the gate, where he was pacing.

"We comin' right back," Malik said over his shoulder.

I just kept on walking.

"Yo, here he come right now," Taxx said.

Malik stopped and turned around.

We could see Chippie striding on the other side of the gate. Had I been strapped, I would have shot him on principle alone. I knew he was armed. And dangerous.

"See," Malik said. "It's only ten more points, man. C'mon, this'll be quick."

"His walk don't look funny to you?" I asked.

Chippie was moving quickly to an inaudible beat. Every time his right leg swung back, there was a dip in his stride, an uneven gallop. Whatever was weighted against his right thigh was not good news for Malik. But my cousin still couldn't see it.

"The nigga just pissed, that's all," he said.

Chippie came to a hole in the gate and began sauntering his way through the opening. The right pocket of his nylon sweats hung low as he wriggled through.

"Shit!" Malik exclaimed.

We turned around and walked away as inconspicuously as possible. To think about it, we must have made quite a sight. Just walking away from the game right then and there, without so much as an explanation.

"Hey!" the sore loser called. "Where ya'll going?"

The only response we could think of was to push an open palm toward our audience like diplomats acknowledging something, without giving it much thought.

"What the fuck was all that about?" Malik asked.

We were passing through the long alley that ran

alongside building 812. It was the only passageway connecting the courts with the front of the projects. Malik spoke as if we were past the danger, but I wasn't taking any chances.

"Just move," I told him.

"Man, motherfuckers can't take it that someone better than them, that's what it is. Sheeit, I wasn't even in top form today. And those kids back there sucked. They wasn't giving me no support. Especially that chubby light-skinned kid—you know who I'm talking about?"

"Uh-huh," I said, even though I had no real idea what he was saying. He may have asked me the riddle of the Sphinx and would have gotten the same answer.

"Man, I shoulda brought some of my boys from school with me. We woulda served they sorry asses. Watch next time— "

"There ain't gonna be no next time," I said, picking up the pace. I began to feel claustrophobic. The passageway seemed longer than ever and it had begun to get dark—too early for the lights to come on, but late enough to make shadows seem funny.

"Yeah, you right," Malik said. "You see how I shut that nigga down?"

BLOWE! The crack erupted.

Malik and I set off like we had springs in our calves and jets in our soles. We used to race each other down the street when we were much younger. Malik would always beat me hands down. But that night, I was showing more hee' than he was.

He tripped over his own fear and stumbled to the ground. He seemed willing to stay there when I bent over to him.

"C'mon," I said. "He don't want us that bad. He just wanna scare us and save his pride. But if we wait around here, best ta believe we gettin' shot."

We got up and continued. The bullets kept coming, bouncing off the wall, sparking against the ground, or disappearing into the night.

The corridor opened into one of the parking lots. We saw the Cutlass, stripped down on cinder blocks, and hopped in it, shutting the doors quietly behind us. Malik rested out across the backseat. The driver and passenger seats were gone, so I laid on the hard frame. Screws and bolts dug into my unprotected skin.

Chippie's footsteps came slapping through the lot. We heard him stop, swear, then laugh before turning around.

I giggled when I was sure it was safe. "Ain't that some funny shit?"

When Malik didn't reply, the sounds of the bullets replayed in my mind. I thought about the non-ricocheting shots that disappeared into the night. The pool of blood growing on the side of his ribs made it known that Chippie's bad aim was really my wishful thinking.

Malik has since spent his days on a hospital bed or in a wheelchair. Three shots had entered his back. One caught his spine.

"Any higher and he could have been quad-" the surgeon said after the operation. He

56

made it sound like there was some great victory in that, or as if that simple bit of knowledge was supposed to make you sit in wonder at the marvels of modern science.

As for Chippie, he was found hanging by a noose from the basketball rim three nights after the shooting.

I swear I don't know how he got there. Still, as much as I'd like to, I can't say that I didn't have anything to do with his death.

So that's the story behind me and my car. After everything happened, she was still in the lot, raped and abandoned. I felt as if I owed her something—she had saved our lives after all. I pulled my resources and got her into working condition over the course of two seasons. An old loveseat in the back, a pair of Lexus chairs up front (Michael said they came from Jordan's father's coupe—I'm not sure if he's kidding), a set of fuzzy dice and she's mine. She's not as fancy as anything Michael pushes, but she gets the job done.

As the engine warms up, I pull the Colt from its nest and slip it beneath my seat, coming up with a fifth of Hennessey. I take a swig.

First shot of the day. It burns my chest. I pass it to Steve.

Ronnie lights a cigarette in the backseat and I begin to choke.

"What the fuck are you doin' man?!" I yell, waving my hands about ferociously.

"I forgot," Ronnie laughs. "You sensitive an' shit."

I roll down my window to push out the last of the nicotine smoke as Ronnie puts out the cancer stick.

"Y'all taking them checks to Beemer?" I ask.

"Of course," Steve cozes.

Beemer's family had moved into one of the houses surrounding the projects shortly after Michael went upstate. He was an odd kid with a thin nose and short crew cut. His head was shaped like an egg lying on its side and his smile resembled the letter *V*. We all thought he was a funny-lookin' Puerto Rican until one day Ronnie, Steve, and I went over to his house and stumbled over our tongues trying to pronounce his last name. After butchering his Polish family honor, we christened him Beemer.

Beemer didn't have any business in West Grove, but liked to come around anyway. He liked hanging around us because he could get girls with us. We liked hanging around him for the same reason—they thought he was Puerto Rican, too.

I remember the day he got his first computer. He called us down into his basement and unveiled a hunkering piece of metal with a cold green cursor blinking at us with authority.

"My mom said I could either get this or get my teeth fixed," Beemer said. He pulled his lip back with his index fingers to show the bulges of two impacted incisors.

The instructions for the computer were thrown out with the box. Beemer never used instructions. He said that they slowed him down, kept him

58

from entering the logic of the machine and its creator, whatever that meant.

His ascension through the ranks of white-collar crime began shortly thereafter. In the sixth grade, he was doctoring report cards. By the time we entered high school, none of us had to worry about running home to beat cutting cards. Steve had even worked in a bank for six months off of a phony diploma before failing a mandatory drug test.

Any court in the land would say that we took advantage of a young boy's need to fit in and perverted his ivory genius to our own ebony ends. But in truth, Beemer reveled in the ability to bend technology to his will and would have done so with or without us. Actually, we were somewhat scared of him—he had all the makings of a mad scientist.

He shared grand visions of the future where computers reigned supreme and viewed himself, and the hand-picked acolytes he would train, as the coming age's witchdoctors. He and his order would travel what was left of the globe, purging evil spirits from computers and making sure that the heartless mechanisms were held at bay.

We all thought he was crazy until we learned all about computer viruses during a field trip to a Learning Center. The instructors were expounding on their contradictory "state-of-the-art" technology, but it was all shit Beemer had schooled us in years before.

FOR THE LOVE OF THIS

Beemer's bent over his laptop computer and doesn't even look up from the screen bouncing colors off his face when we walk in. To his right is a printer about the size of a stereo system pushing out what looks like W-2 forms. Though I've never filled out any taxes in my life, I've seen Ma smudge and tweak the figures on her 1040s many a Spring morning.

A clean, neat nervous type in a suit is looking over his shoulder. I'd have to describe his look as dainty more than sharp, flashy, almost feminine.

The basement is filled with boxes of electronic equipment, papers and books scattered about like autumn leaves. A futon and a couch stare at each other across the small rectangular coffee table covered with magazines with names like *Tech Word* and *Computer's Digest*.

In addition to the laptop, there are two desktops, spread out across a cafeteria table. The larger consoles are hooked up to multiple oversized monitors that rest in shelves attached to the wall, like the TV display in a large electronics store. A soft light slides in between the blinds of the small windows and reflects off the screens.

"Job's done! Job's done!" One of the computers bark. An animated bird on the screen stares at me. Then it bulges its eyes and squeaks its large beak. "Job's done! Job's done!"

Beemer snatches the printouts and hands them to the dainty fellow.

"Are you sure this is gonna work?" he asks.

"Never failed yet." Beemer smiles, raising his shoulders and offering his hands like a man who has nothing to hide.

Beemer's assertion doesn't seem to calm the man's nerves any. Regardless, he looks around the room and tries to sound hip when he leaves. "Be cool, homeboys."

Ronnie checks the CD burners in the corner before sitting on the couch.

"Why does dubbing these video games take so damned long?" he asks.

"Because there's so many more bytes of information on them than a music disc, when you load up the . . ." Beemer says, before realizing it was a rhetorical question.

I take a seat next to Ronnie. He pulls out a cigar and unwraps its leaf like he's undressing a lost lover. It's then fileted, its innards dumped into a small wastebasket. Ronnie takes one of the two plastic jars from the coffee table and removes a sticky bud of florescent green marijuana. After crumbling it into the cigar paper, he smiles deliciously. The other jar is unscrewed and relieved of a healthy portion of black weed.

"This is lower back pain medicine," he grins.

One thing about Ronnie, he knows his herbs. Whether you have a cold, you're tired, or you just want that extra zip in tonight's episode, Ronnie knows the right mixture to get you going. He says that he can smoke all he wants, because he has combinations of trees that will keep his lungs functioning properly.

Once I couldn't remember the combination to my gym locker and he rolled me a joint of "memory potion." Two tokes later, I not only remembered the combination, but everything I needed to know for my earth science quiz as well. Since then, I've been using his mixtures to get women to tell the truth, make music, and keep prolonged erections.

There's a knock at the door. Steve comes back with a pleasant African fellow who introduces himself as Bak'tu. Bak'tu hands Beemer a worn envelope full of ragged money.

"Okay," Beemer says, "who was the twelfth president of the United States?"

"Lyndon B. Johnson?" Bak'tu smiles.

"Close enough," Beemer laughs. He hands Bak'tu a large manila envelope. "Congratulations. You are now a legal citizen of the finest country in the world." Then, "Don't be stupid."

"Free enterprise," Beemer gleams when Bak'tu is gone. "It's the American way."

"Beemer, they got a special file on you at the FBI," I joke. I tell him about the show I saw on cable last night. It said something about micro chips the size of a grain of rice being used to track dogs and livestock. If they could do that to dogs, who's to say they weren't tracking all of this stolen merchandise down here?

"Man, you niggas caught on to universal truths and called them conspiracy theories," Beemer laughs. "It's pure propaganda. Just like parades, the news, and wars. They're just trying to scare you. The funny thing is that the truth is way more scarier than that bullshit you see on the tel-lie-vision, man. If they were to put the real technology on the tel-lie-vision, it would send you simple motherfuckers into a panic. Tel-lie-vision: They keep telling lies to your vision."

He leans back in his swivel chair, content that he's made a point. He pulls a cellular phone off his desk. "Oh, I been meaning to give this to you, man."

He tosses me the phone.

"I took care of this one myself," he says with that wide *V* smile. "It's a special project. I made up a whole new sequence for cellular phone numbers. Given the market's current rate of growth, it'll be about four or five years before they even realize that these numbers are being used . . . Unless, you want to think it has a stir-fried rice tracer in there or something." He laughs.

I take the phone with a smirk.

"Yeah, that's the XT-88," Beemer says. "Does everything—organizer with time/date schedule, alarm clock, calculator, you name it. It even has the daily conversion rates for francs, pounds, yen, all that shit."

Ronnie passes me the blunt. The smoke burns my throat and fills my lungs on the first toke.

"Well, then find out how much sixteen hundred and eighty-three dollars and forty-seven cent in Social Security checks is worth at my twenny-five percent commission," Steve says, tallying up the checks across the table.

"Why don't you get down with us, D?" Ronnie asks.

"Diamond don't need none of this," Beemer says. "He's a big rapper, man. He's gonna be making more money than all of us. And it's gonna be all legal, right?"

"That's not what I heard," chimes Steve. "I heard he ain't got no time for us 'cause he's rolling with the crew that's too strong to think."

The second toke scorches my chest and explodes in my head.

"You still working with them knuckleheads— Gage and Mr. B?" Beemer asks. "Fuck Gage and fuck Mr. B—they ain't shit. All that shit they doing is stupid. When they get caught—and believe me, they will get caught 'cause they're all pinheads— they throwing all their dumb asses under the jail. If I, by some chance, wake up stupid and get caught, they're giving me a job on the federal payroll."

"They gonna have us dropping bombs on Saddam and shit." Ronnie gleams.

I push out a large cloud of smoke through my nostrils.

"We roll like family," says Beemer. "When one man eats, everyone eats.You don't see me pushing a phat whip and my boys walking, do you?"

"Yeah," Ronnie giggles. "We're all walking."

"All that material shit is gonna go down soon anyway," Steve says. "The hustle is gonna change. When 2000 come, anyone who ain't in the know-how on the tech side is gonna be ass out. Yeah, niggas is always gonna wanna get high, have niggas killed or whatever, but all that gangsterism is gotta change. The game won't be the same."

Last toke.

"You know something about you, Diamond?" Steve asks. He rests on his knees and comes in close; he has something important to say. "You remind me of Colossus."

"Colossus?" asks Ronnie. "From the X-Men?"

"Yeah," says Steve. " 'Cause you know that nigga's an artist, too, right?—he's a painter. You ain't never see the time he was in love with Callisto?"

I give one of those spacy, but attentive nods that you can give only when you're zoning and paying deep attention at once. There's something called parapsychicism, or close to that, where whatever happens on the physical plane takes place on psychic levels as well. Like a bird flying high in the sky ain't really a bird, but a guide or an avatar through different realities. Well, there's some parapsychic shit going on right now, 'cause Steve ain't really Steve.

"Anyway," he continues, "Colossus can turn his flesh into nigh invulnerable steel, right? So here you have this guy who likes to paint, some real soft shit, but he has an exterior that no one can get through. And he's always going through some self-analytical shit about it, like, 'I really want to paint flowers,' and all this shit, but here's the clincher—the guy been saving the world since I could read, right? Turning to steel and all this shit, but he still can't do that shit in stages. It's like he's either pink flesh that's susceptible to a paper cut, or he's this metal guy that can take a missile to the chest. No graduation." Steve puts his hands out like a king bestowing frankincense and myrhh on the child in Bethlehem. "Ya heard?"

Yeah, I think I hear more than he knows he's saying.

"Okay, okay—back to reality." Beemer lets out tendrils of smoke from his nose. "The stuff I'm doing now is gonna position us for the new millenium," he says proudly. "The change has already happened. It's just that our minds can't accept it all at once, so it comes to us in waves. Give it till like, 2002, 2003, everyone's gonna wake up. But, like the Chinese say, you can't build a well when you're thirsty, 'cause then it's already too late, y'know?"

"The Chinese say that, eh?" I question.

"Umm-humm," he nods. "Or something like that."

The room laughs.

The smoke makes my head wide, giving my thoughts room to swim. Steve's words reverb in my head—*graduation, invulnerable steel; susceptible.* Sacrificing my exterior to make my art live.

Dancing like no one's watching.

It's a minute before I give pause to digest Beemer's worldview. I don't know about his doomsday prophecies and all that, but I know that he's right about one thing—messing with Michael and Mr. B is not going to lead anywhere but a five-by-seven with three squares a day. Jail is someplace I'm not trying to see.

When I come back to normal space and time, Ronnie and Steve are leading Lara Croft on another mission courtesy of the PlayStation. I grab a pen and pad from Beemer's desk. The words jump out of me.

I got more schemes than I got teams / Mad cliques with tricks up their sleeves / From credit card scams to moving trees / Nigga, please / You don't want it when I'm blunted / Your whole crew'll get confronted / Scope out the prime opponent for his Christ piece / Make him run it / Quick flash of the four-fifth Escape in the Eight-fifth' / Or the five hundred / Starsky and Hutch on our tail / Yo Gage, gun it . . .

No.

Who wanna test these? / Nigga please / I'll smack your testes like Gabrielle Reese / Flip you like Surya Bonaly / You're not mon ami / You're an enemy.

No.

Live life like a prayer / Clothes don't make the player / Spin the bottle, truth or dare / Necking the closet when the game was fair / Now the devil's got a virus in the lair / So I wear a layer / Out of love not fear / Something for you to hear clear / There's a killer in every man, so beware / And stay aware / Before you find yourself far from here / Talking to a white man with a white beard in a white chair.

When I stop writing it's past five o'clock. Shit, I forgot about Tamara.

SuperTracks is a small but fully equipped studio across town in Bed Stuy. Its owner, Marshall Stanton, is a Vietnam vet, but not like most other vets—all disgruntled and stuff. Nah, Marshall's different. He doesn't bitch about veterans' rights, join in any protest or any of that other stuff. He always says, "They caught me when I was young and stupid" and leaves it at that.

I figure you have to grow up hard and quick in war, so that may explain why he's part cop, part big brother, and part father in the most disciplinary ways possible. He doesn't talk much about anything—the war, especially—that's not directly related to the running of SuperTracks, and even then it's short and sweet. What I do know of his wartime activities was gleaned from our conversations at dumb o'clock in the morning, when the only things awake were the alley cats.

After being on the wrong end of one too many raids and ambushes from the Viet Cong, he began to wonder why he was fighting and who he was fighting for. He says the enemy fought with too much conviction for their cause to be anything other than righteous. Still, he was a soldier. He followed his orders because he had to. And because he wanted to get out alive.

When he came home, "I realized that if you keep taking orders from someone else, you're working to make their dreams come true," he said once. "And if you keep making other people's dreams come true, you ain't got nothing left for yourself but nightmares."

He secured loans and borrowed money to build up the studio, one piece at a time, providing quality recording at breakneck prices. Not only is SuperTracks like an artistic haven for cats like me, it's legendary. Everyone's recorded there. Everyone. Still Marshall never asks for finder's fees, royalty points, or anything of the sort. He runs the studio for meager profit, and that's that.

I enter the studio at dusk, my backpack full of tapes and pages, making my way to Catherine, the receptionist, with a smile.

"I thought you were coming in early today," she says, pushing her glasses up on her nose.

"This is early," I smile back at her.

"Marshall must really love you," she shakes her head playfully.

I walk down the hallway. The walls are adorned with plaques and awards of all sorts—from community organizations and the recording industry alike. It sometimes strikes me to walk down this hall of fame. Everyone says the day is soon coming when I'll have a gold or platinum plaque to squeeze in with the others, but that day seems so far off. I can't even get my demo finished, much less sell one million records.

Halfway down the corridor, I hear the sounds of the song I've been working on for the past week.

I stop and listen to it as if for the first time.

Are there enough highs, enough lows? . . . That

couplet needs to be ran through stronger . . . The hook is tight but it needs some scratches. Maybe if I used that old Sugarhill Record and—

The music stops abruptly.

I rush into the studio. Baz is ass up, fiddling underneath the soundboard. He stands up, and stares blankly at the blinking lights and fluctuating levels. He flips a switch. Nothing. Another switch. Still nothing. A third switch lets off a round of feedback that would scare a banshee.

"What the fuck?!" I yell.

Surprised, Baz whips around to see me. His curly hair sticks up like an overdone perm, his eyes bulge, you could fit two of him inside of his outfit—he looks like El Casper, the Hip-Hop Ghost.

"I don't know what the fuck happened, man!" He shouts over the speakers' wailing, turning back to the control panel, twisting various knobs in vain efforts to correct the problem. Finally, the room goes silent. I notice the irritated redness of his nose, the dash of white powder stuck to the outside of his left nostril. He catches on quickly, wiping at his nose self-consciously and putting forth lame excuses.

"I told you this shit is fucked up, man. Worthless. All shorted wires and broken knobs. Marshall needs to get some real equipment in here. We can't work with——"

"Save that shit." I've heard all of his excuses ad infinitum. If it wasn't the equipment, it was the wiring. When it wasn't the wiring, it was the mics. Or the levels, or something else. And to top it all off, he's back to sniffing coke. Now I see why he's been on top of me to get paid. He has a habit to support.

"The board was working fine yesterday," I say. "You're supposed to be a damned engineer and you can't even work a simple soundboard."

"I'm telling you, man. This shit is fucked up." He crouches down underneath the console and resumes fumbling around. "There," he insists, coming up over the board. He flips the master switch.

Nothing.

"Hold on," he mumbles, guessing at the knobs like a game of Old Maid.

I calmly reach over, flip a lever, turn a dial to the right.

The music kicks out in full force.

"Man, when I went to school, we trained on the good shit," he says. "This ancient shit, I don't know about. Now, if we had a digital board, with the presets and programmable memory, I could . . ."

I'm not sure what to think. Marshall's equipment isn't state of the art, but it's far from trash. And it's available for cheap. Baz is more trouble than he's worth at times, but I can't afford to get another engineer. Fuck, I can barely pay for the studio time, even with the breaks that Marshall is giving me.

I gave my all for this country and what do I have to show for it? Twelve pieces of shrapnel embedded in my person, which the doctors say are not worth retrieving, an arm which is equal parts Teflon and bone, nightmares where I waltz with

71

decapitated bodies in a waterfall of blood and limbs, and an unending ringing in my left ear which prevents me from fully enjoying any of the music created in my own studio. Still, I should be glad I haven't dropped—and I do mean dropped—dead like so many of the others. Hendricks, Jones, Coltrane, Young, and Wallace all died of "old-age" a bit too early for my blood. And all in the past eight months.

Medals of honor, Purple Hearts—you name it, we got 'em. But none of that could secure us decent employment. And it sure as hell doesn't give us amnesty from death.

Decorated soldiers dying young. And broke. Were I a conspiracy theorist, many things would come to mind. But I know the truth; I was there.

There was no concerted effort to eliminate the Black race and perhaps they did, as some say, experiment upon us without our knowing. But I don't believe the government's intentions were anywhere near as diabolical as some of these crackpots and overzealous news magazines would have the world believe. The fact of the matter is that we were sacrificed in the name of science and war, curiosity and greed, audacity and pride. Democracy and the greater good were just smoke screens for the actions of men who were not as evil as they were selfish.

A lot of men died in that war—Black, white, and other. The slaughter was indifferent. The only ones who dare not call it a war are the ones who were not there, who didn't hear the cries, who didn't wake up cursing God for giving them another day in liege with the Devil; the ones who did not see their friends-turned-family sliced, diced, evaporated, turned into a smoking mass of blood and entrails. And every minute, you couldn't help but wonder when it would be your turn.

I still wonder.

When I built this studio, I wanted nothing more than to give these kids a chance. I didn't want them coming face to face with this country's lies like I did. Nothing as self-serving as seeing my name in lights, cavorting with stars or gallivanting the globe. No, my purposes were more grandiose, delusional even. I thought I could save a generation. Or, at least, scoop a handful of kids from death's gaping maw; provide a door number two to those military recruiting offices, luring them in with polished smiles, shiny shoes, and white lies.

Maybe I've done my part. Perhaps I've aided a chosen few along in their pursuit of happiness and my work here is done. I have to be honest—I really can't compete with the newer studios; they have the higher-end technology that the kids want. I can continue to undercut their prices, but bargains and reputation can only take me but so far. Plus, I'm doing a dead-man's float in bills— there's the overdue electric bill, the telephone is on shut-off notice, I'm behind on my lease, the bank loans, everything. Slashing my prices would only bring me deeper into debt.

At least if I could get the board in studio B up I would be able to book more time, and maybe, hopefully, get some more funds coming in.

And then I can't even think about my domestic situation.

My head hurts. Bad.

And I'm not referring to the chronic low-level throb that follows me closer than my own shadow. It's the stress. The medicine they gave me in 'Nam was heavily based in morphine and proved to be nothing more than a gateway drug. Dean, McRae, Hunsten, and Piplovytch never got that angry, greedy, chattering monkey off their backs. I watched them rot slowly from the organs out, to the point where they were more like parasites than men, like a mouse kissed by a tarantula.

I swear, I'll never get hooked on anything, not even the prescribed painkillers ever again. Never.

But I need something.

I open the small drawer on my desk, fumbling around for my bottle of Tylenol. The hand grip of my .35 just falls, leaps, or runs into my palm. I'm caressing it before I even notice it's in my hand.

Its bright chrome pulses florescent when I pull it from its hiding place.

I give the revolver's cylinder a twirl. It moves slow; I don't like the sound of it—figure I'll have to oil it up tonight. I've never used it, but Grandma Stanton always told me it's better to have and not need than to need and not have, and Mama ain't raise no fools. But, perhaps more importantly in this equation, it was Sergeant Lucas who said, "The wrong time to check your weapon is when you smell the rice on one of these gook's breath."

The intercom rings. It gives me a bit of comfort to know that I'm able to pay my receptionist.

"Yes, Catherine."

"I have Master Mix's manager on the phone."

Corey's a snake, but he's one of my best paying customers. He only calls when he needs a favor. Wonder what it is this time.

"Put him through."

Click-click.

"Corey Colt, what's shaking?" I ask, unsuspiciously as I can.

"Not much, playboy. Not much. How's it hanging?"

"Barely. What can I do for you?"

"Well, you know, Mix has this certified banger he needs to put down, but we just booked a last-minute gig. We're gonna have to push tomorrow's session to tonight."

"Can't do it. I already have some kids in here for the night."

"Well," Corey says and I can almost hear his belly moving across the grass, "when a man says he can't do something, all I hear is that I haven't given him a figure he can live with."

I look over the bills in front of me. Corey's words slither out of the silence and into my ear.

"Is three thousand good for the night, or do I have to bring the whole checkbook?"

Three thousand? I can get the board fixed for that much.

"Give me an hour," I say before I realize it.

"Okay," Corey says. "See you in half an hour."

The line goes dead.

I dangle the receiver in my hand before making the call.

"Diamond? I need to talk to you in my office."

I'm just putting the gun away when he enters.

"What's up Marshall?" Diamond asks with that smile he has that says he's guilty of something.

I motion for him to sit down.

"How's it going in there?"

"Oh, the noise? Well, we were just having problems with the levels and—"

That explains the smile.

"Never mind that, Diamond. How long have you got before you finish your demo?"

"I don't know. Maybe another two songs or so. You know my shit gotta be right, Marshall. I ain't about to throw any old bullshit out there."

"Hmm . . ."

"What's going on?" he asks.

He's really a good kid. Works hard. Every time he comes in here. One of the most diligent workers I've seen in years. Man, if I could instill this kid's ethic into some of my paying customers, I wouldn't even have to come in anymore. Catherine could just let them in, answer the phones, and tell them to lock up when they leave.

"I'm sorry, Diamond," I sigh a bad wind, "but you've got to wrap it up for the night."

"Wrap it up? But I just got here."

"I've got another group coming in about a half hour," I say.

I pick up the bills from my desk; shuffle them around, write a note to myself, find something interesting in *Archie Bunker's Place*, which is playing on the small black-and-white set to my right—anything not to look in his eyes. He's a real heartbreaker, this one. I see why all the girls go crazy for him.

"Yo, that's fucked up Marshall. You should have just told me you had another session booked."

"It's not like I knew about this ahead of time. These other guys, they just called a few minutes ago."

I fold my arms across my chest. Build up my resolve. Protect my heart. Never let them see you sweat. Another lesson from 'Nam: Show no pity—*even if she's the most fragile little thing you've ever seen, show no pity until her heart isn't beating. Then you check her crotch for razor blades to see if you have to make an extra prayer tonight.*

"And just like that and you're telling me to pack up my shit and clear out?"

"Look, these guys are cash-paying customers," I reply, more serious now. *Show no pity.*

Aside from the darts in his eyes that would make King Cobra blink, he has no reply. Leaves the office. Quietly. He's upset as shit, but still has respect.

Sorry, Diamond.

Show no pity.

The words *cash paying* are still burning my ears when Baz and I are making our way out of the studio.

Marshall's greeting a group of people at the entrance. I instantly recognize Master Mix from his videos. He's wearing a custom outfit of butter-soft leather and a matching hat, both showing his insignia—two *M*'s inside of twelve-inch records. Following close behind are three women in skintight minis and an assortment of hangers-on and wanna-bes, buzzing all around Master Mix, talking him up. Some mover-and-shaker type in a perfectly cut three-piece suit is leading the way.

"Christ, don't you guys ever sleep?" Marshall says to the mover-and-shaker with a laugh. He leads the entourage toward the studio and past me and Baz without so much as a glance.

"Later, Marshall," I say, but I'm not sure why. I really want to say something else, something like *Fuck you Marshall, you're just a . . . a . . . a . . .* But that's the problem. I have no beef with Marshall. Even though I feel I should.

He turns around, almost as an afterthought.

"I'll get you some more time tomorrow, Diamond," he says, waving his hand dismissively.

"Yo, brother, we ain't cuttin' in to your time, now are we?" Master Mix asks earnestly.

Oh shit. Master Mix is talking to me.

"Nah," I say. "It's cool."

"You sure, now?" One of the women smiles. I know that look that she's giving me.

Maybe another time, love. Right now I'm kind of pissed, being tossed out on my ass and all—you do understand.

"Hey man, why you ain't tell us you had another brother in the house?" Mix says to Marshall. "Hey, you guys can come sit in on our session, if you want. It's cool."

Oh shit. Master Mix is inviting me to his studio session.

"Don't sweat it, Mix," the three-piece suit says. "I'm sure they were just hanging out. Right, Marshall?"

I pause a moment for Marshall's answer, but then decide I don't want to hear it. I tug Baz and dither out into the street.

A black Ford Bronco screeches up beside us as we're getting into the Cutlass.

I instinctively go for my Colt.

The Bronco shines like chrome-dipped obsidian, its radio emitting chest-shattering bass thumps that shake the mirrors of my ride.

The sonic assault ends as the engine cuts and Michael emerges from the driver's side.

He's a walking billboard, decked from head to toe with large brand-name logos. Even his socks bear a high-fashion crest. The heavy load of gold around his neck, wrists, and fingers clang with his movements.

"Where the fuck you going, bro?" he asks. "I thought you said you were going to be here all night!"

"We got bumped," I say matter of factly.

"Bumped?" he snarls. "What the fuck is on soldier boy's mind?"

Baz pipes up, "Yeah, Gage. That's what I'm talking about—"

"You shut the fuck up before I smack your Spic ass back to Guantanamera," Michael declares. Then, as if hit by a lightning bolt of realization,

"Don't your ass owe me some money?" He fingers at his smelling piece informatively.

Now I know where Baz has been getting his nose candy.

"Diamond! Diamond!"

It's the three-piece suit, gallumphing out of the studio.

"I'm so glad I caught up to you," he gushes, breathing heavily. "I had no idea who you were back there." He pauses and gathers himself. "Listen, playboy, I'm Corey Colt, Master Mix's manager."

He sticks out a business card, which Michael intercepts.

"He already got a manager."

"And that would be you?"

"I ain't the fuckin' tooth fairy."

"Well," Corey says, "I think my reputation speaks for itself." He hands me another card. "Call me. We'll do lunch."

He skelters back into the studio.

"Can you believe that motherfucker?" Michael laughs. "He must not know how we get down. Anyway, now that these niggas done kicked you to the curb, what am I supposed to do with them?"

I look into the Bronco and notice that we have an audience: three girls with exaggerated pouts.

"Well, it's three of us and three of them," Baz suggests.

Michael quickly grabs Baz's nose between his index and middle fingers, digging the sharp edges of his rings into my engineer's flesh.

"Ain't I tell you to shut up?"

Michael rips his hand away, leaving Baz's nose bleeding.

"Man, I can't believe these motherfuckers bumped you on some *Gong Show* shit. Over that tired-ass Master Mix?"

He answers his rhetorical question by producing a shiny derringer from his sock.

A derringer. I'm startled at the sight of the weapon. A derringer is smaller than a .25 and only holds two shots; but those two shots will hit you with the force of a .9 millimeter at close range. It's a business weapon and should only be used as such, or as a backup to your main gun. Michael's back up to his main gun is its twin.

Why the derringer? Is it to impress the girls or something deeper?

"Man, fuck them motherfuckers, thinkin' shit is sweet," he growls. "Don't nobody fuck with my artist."

"Yo, watch that," I step toward him quickly. I know Michael—the only time to stop him is before he starts.

"This ain't no street shit," I say. "This is my fuckin' career. How many times I gotta tell you to leave that Dirty Harry shit out of this?"

We eyeball each other briefly.

"A-ight," he grins. "Burger King, motherfucker—have it your way."

He reconceals the small weapon and wraps his arm around me.

"You just lucky. Never know when a little gun like this is gonna save your life," he giggles.

81

Save my life? Something's going on with Michael.

"C'mon," he says, before I can get out a question, "I want you to meet these shorties I caught last night. You see Jeannine's in the front seat, so you know she's special."

The car smells of a perfumed fruit called aphrodisia. It turns me on.

I give Jeannine the once over. When Michael says a girl is "special," it means that she's his, broken in and trained to tell the boldest lie or keep the deepest secret without batting an eyelash. Samson used the jawbone of an ass to strike down a thousand Philistines, and Michael knows that a loose-lipped woman is a much more destructive weapon.

Jeannine's mouth isn't the only tight part of her anatomy. Filled in all the right places, she could pass for a homegirl in *Essence*: milky light skin, hair and nails done enough to show class, but not so much as to cover up her 'tude. Her jeans are painted on like a second skin and her low-cut tank top accentuates her cleavage.

Debbie and Keisha, the two in the backseat, were full-bodied as well—a bit more crude and homegrown, but inviting nonetheless. (What a friend Michael is, offering me a selection.)

We pass what appears to be idle chatter, but they're unwittingly filling out applications for the Diamond St. James Sweepstakes, where the grand prize is, well, Diamond St. James—if only for one night.

Debbie's studying to be a paralegal, is an aethiest, and would be a weeping willow. Keisha's a cashier at a pharmacy, thinks the Bible is the unabridged word of God, and doesn't know much about trees except that they have that holiday for them right before everyone goes back to school.

Keisha wins the lottery—I can't fuck with no chick that don't believe in God.

I pass her my cell phone digits, tell her we'll meet up later tonight at the Barracuda Lounge.

"Yeah, I'ma be there," I say. "Why am I gonna tell you to meet me if I ain't gonna be there?"

Hmmm . . . Maybe I can make Debbie a believer.

When I get home, the aroma of Ma's dinner cooking and the melody of an obscure Marvin Gaye tune fill our small apartment. Food and music—I know I can always count on that when I walk through my door.

Ma fixes me a heaping plate of spaghetti and meatballs. The sauce is thick and chunky with hearty cuts of peppers, onions, leek, and scallions. Though the ingredients are no-frills, Ma puts enough elbow grease and love into the dish's preparation to make it rank with Little Italy's best.

I dig into it voraciously, grab seconds, and wash the chipped dishes with diluted soap before jumping in the shower.

"Tamara called," Ma says when I'm in my room, drying off.

I debate whether or not to return her call.

If I do, there's sure to be a lot of back and forth,

hemming and hawing, griping and groaning. I've been working in the studio for most of the past week and a night at the Barracuda would do me well. But Tamara is patient and she does deserve, at the least, a phone call for standing her up earlier. I'm about to call her up when the cellular begins with its digital chirping.

Beep-briiing. Beep-briiing. Beep-briiing.

"Hey Diamond," purrs the soft voice on the other end. "You know who this is?"

It's Keisha.

WATCHU WANNA DO?

The lines outside the Barracuda snake around the block, with its patrons separated by genders like a Jewish wedding.

I look at these chumps trying to get in—throngs of them, attired in ghetto regalia from the highest fashions to the Fulton Avenue knockoffs. Pitiful.

I stand apart from them 'cause my outfit was made by no other than Tamara Lewis—tailored farmer's jeans, a yellow linen shirt with matching skullcap to cover up my unraveling do. Nondescript, low-key, classy.

I make my way to the doors.

"My man, Diamond St. James," one of the bouncers says.

He knows my name. I know his face. I don't care as long as I get in quick and for free.

Inside, the club reeks of musky cologne and sweet sweat. In a world of puppeteers and puppets, the Barracuda Lounge is where all the strings become entangled in intricate webs of power. The cocktail tables of this meat market decide magazine covers, chart positions, and record deals more than corporate conference tables and the market place. It's where the crime world and the music industry converge for orgies of coquettes who sling lines for monies and cokeheads who sniff lines for funnies.

I peer out over the crowd, sipping on a White Russian at the bar.

"Yo, Diamond. What the fuck is up, man?" Beemer smiles widely, angling next to me at the bar.

Ronnie and Steve come around him, materializing like ghosts from thin air.

"So you think about what I said earlier?" Beemer asks, after ordering himself a screwdriver.

"What's that?"

We have to yell in each other's ears to combat the music.

"About my offer, you know, getting down with the program."

"Oh, you were serious."

"Hell, yeah," Beemer nods, gulping down the last of his highball.

"I'm thinkin' 'bout it, then."

"Yeah, well keep thinking. The door is open for you. There's a lot you can bring to the table—you have smarts and know-how, man. Plus we could make a killing off your music industry contacts alone. Ronnie could keep them high and you could keep them connected."

I laugh and sip my Russian. The ice is melting, watering it down, so I decide to finish it off with a mighty swig.

"I got this plan, man," Beemer continues. "If I can get into one record label and reconfigure their computer system—all them motherfuckers will come to me. And that's good, *legal* money. One big job can have you set for a month."

We order another round of drinks. I listen intently.

"Anyone you bring to me, you get a commission off of. And if they refer anyone to me, you get a cut of that, too. Man, I'm talking stock options—"

Just then, Michael comes in like the proverbial bull in a china shop and dismantles our small meeting.

"*Arrivederci*, motherfucker," he says to Beemer.

"I keep telling your ignorant ass, I ain't Italian. I'm Polish."

"Well, then, get the fuck outski."

"You know what, Gage? You one dumb, ignorant motherfucker."

"About to get dumber on your ass—"

"Like I'm scared, dude." Beemer grills him long enough to let Michael know. Then he turns to me.

"Think about that shit, D." He walks away with Steve and Ronnie, the three disappearing into a sea of dancing bodies.

"So wassup, son?" Michael asks, as if nothing happened.

He seems a bit nervous. Actually, more upset than nervous. He wants to kill Beemer—this I know for sure. It's almost as if Michael's jealous of our relationship.

With good reason, most people are scared of

Michael, moreover, Gage. Michael thrives offa fear. Beemer hasn't ever, and probably never will, lose a moment's sleep over Michael. But his computer wizardry makes him an invaluable asset to Mr. B. Plain and simple, he's untouchable.

"Why you always gotta shit on people?" I ask him.

"Fuck Beemski, I'll make a kielbasa out of his ass." He smiles, but sees I'm not laughing.

"Don't go getting all sensitive on me, now." He slides his arms around me. "I got those bitches right there." I follow his line of sight to a small booth, where Jeannine and Keisha sit nursing drinks. Keisha says something to me with her eyes, then smiles and whispers in Jeannine's ear. They giggle like grade schoolers across a crowded cafeteria.

"Shorty's a straight dime," I say, but Michael can't hear me. He has that same look in his eyes that he had in church all those years ago. I've learned it best not to be around when he gets in that mode.

Oh, fuck. He's scheming on Hollis.

You damned right I was scheming on Hollis! I ain't like that motherfucker one bit. Wasn't shit, anyway—petty-ass dealer, thinkin' he movin' something.

You had to see him, though—surrounded by some tricks and screw-faced cats. Dude was rocking a lime green suit with a yellow shirt and some fake green gators, like he was a pimp or something.

But that ain't the clincher. The clincher was his jewels.

He had this iced-down medallion hanging from a Figueroa link. Ice, ice, baby—I'm talking pure diamonds. There was even more of the glassy stuff on his rings, watch, and bracelet. He had this one ring, look like a little Mount Everest resting on his pinky.

I looked at my jewelry—no glitter, just straight gold.

You know this nigga Gage got vexed.

"That's a $40,000 vic," I said to Diamond. "At least."

"What are you talkin' about?"

"Hollis. I say we catch him sleeping and—" I cocked back an air pistol and let off and *klik-chack* to let Diamond know what was up.

That's when he turned bitch. As usual.

"Who, Hollis?" he cried. "Nigga, you must have lost your mind!"

Sounded like he was part of the Vienna Boys Choir or something. I could see he was gonna take a little convincing. Had to plug into his deepest desire.

"Yo, D, Fort Knox ain't got nothing on that nigga," I said. "His jewels alone is enough to pay for studio time, production equipment, sample clearances—you name it."

I could tell he thought about it for a second. I'll give him that much.

"I ain't down with that," he said. "I love my life too much."

I was still sizing up Hollis a few minutes later when Diamond tapped my shoulder.

"That's William White over there." He pointed to a little rat-faced guy in an expensive suit. There was a bottle of Cristal resting in an ice bucket on the table. The cat was having what seemed to be an intense discussion with some other dude over flutes of champagne. The way the other dude cocked his head and listened to rat face, I knew he was someone important.

But Diamond wanted be an asshole and ain't tell me who the guy was. I know he just wanted me to ask. (He's like that sometimes.) So I did.

"Who's that?"

"He's a top dog—CEO of Platinum Records."

"Word?" I said. Platinum was the hottest label in town.

"Umm-humm," Diamond nodded. "The only one that made more stars than him is God. Man, he could make things happen."

It's shit like that I don't understand about Diamond. I mean, here he was in the same room as one of the most powerful players in the rap game and all he could do was sit there with his jaw wide open, gawking like a freakin' groupie.

I guess that's why he made me his manager.

I looked that little runt up and down and knew his whole card, straight.

But, when I'm heading over there to politic, Diamond wanna hold me back. I had to laugh.

When that nigga Gage do his thing, fools just watch.

*   *   *

Why Michael gotta be so . . . Michael?

I don't need him going over to Will White on no dumbness.

But I can't front: The cat is smooth. He slid through the crowd like a greased eel and now he's chumming up to White.

What's this? Teeth are showing, heads are cocking back—they're having a good time! Michael is over there shooting the breeze with Will White!

I can't believe this.

I'm about to order another drink when Michael signals for me to join them.

Oh shit. I'm about to meet William White.

"See, Mr. White, this is my rap artist that I was telling you about," I hear Michael saying as I get near the table. "He's the next."

"Pleasure to meet you, Diamond." When Mr. White offers me his hand, I can see his clear nail polish shining off the club's lighting.

"Pleasure to meet you too, Mr. White," I say.

Pleasure to meet you too, Mr. White? Did that sound gay? Couldn't I think of anything better? Fuck!

"So, Diamond, your manager here tells me that you're one of the best-kept secrets around here."

"Yeah, well, I guess you could say that."

"Well," White laughs, "how about you let me judge that for myself?"

Michael's prompting me with hand gestures behind White. I have no idea what he expects me to do. Perform? He could've warned me or something.

Too late for all that, though. This is my big chance. I bust a rap into White's ear:

"Tap jaws and leave rap scarred / Make you ask / Has God? Pulled a fast card / When your brain is fracchawed / From the rapt-chaw / When I catch y'all . . ."

I'm building into a tempest when White smiles and shakes his head good-naturedly.

"Only if you have a copy of your demo on you," he says. "I run into a lot of kids who can perform live but can't cut a decent record. I'm not a promoter—I don't sell shows, I sell albums."

"Well . . . I don't have my demo on me right now."

"But we can get it to you," Michael chimes in.

"Can you have it to my office by noon tomorrow?" White asks. "If you're as good as your manager here says you are, we might be able to do some business."

Noon? Tomorrow?

"Well, Mr. White, I really don't have a completed demo tape right now. I'm in the process of finishing one."

Michael quickly jumps in. "It's on the reel Mr. White. It's almost done, and I'm telling you right now, it's hot to death! You know what I'm saying?"

Mr. White seems as if all the interest was just drained out of his body.

"Okay," he says, and shifts his body toward the ass-kisser he was conversing with before Michael interrupted. "Listen boys, I only deal with serious acts. Why don't you and your artist here stay at it and, if you ever complete the tape, give me a call."

Michael takes a hostile step toward White. The mogul is so small that a harsh breath could blow him over. But that doesn't matter.

Out of nowhere, there are two slick-haired bruiser types hovering over Michael. Money can't buy you love, but it can rent loyalty.

"That's it? Give you a call?" Michael spits.

"Yo, don't fade it, Gage," I say and quickly grab his arm. Now is not the time nor place for his temper to flare up. "Let it go, son. That's just how this industry game rolls its dice."

I squeeze his arm tighter to make my point.

"Let it go," I say, shocked at how menacing my voice sounds.

We make our way over to Keisha and Jeannine.

"Oh, y'all finished playing Big Willie?" Jeannine's annoyed.

Michael cuts her a glance and she backs down. Quickly.

Before anyone says a thing, Michael's cell phone rings out.

He answers, puts one hand over his ear to block out the ruckus, speaks a few words, listens for a beat.

"Come on, D," he says getting up from the table. "We gotta make a run."

WHAT, WHAT?
WHAT, WHAT?

We pulled up outside of Tiny's. There's never any security out front, but even the wind couldn't have made it in without Mr. B's approval.

Inside, the old geezers were playing dominoes and cards, puffing on cigars. There was also an unhealthy amount of bones being smoked. I figured all the pollution was messing with Diamond's sinuses, allergies, or whatever his problem is with cigarettes. Too bad. This was business.

Jason was wiping down the bar, looking as old as dirt. Wanda looked even older, circulating with a tray full of drinks. I figure at some point, he was the good-looking bartender who helped everyone with their problems and she was that sexy waitress everyone wanted to take home. Yeah, at some point long ago, that may have been the case.

We passed the relics with nods of acknowledgment and made our way to the back. At a corner table, JT, Tin, Tyrone, and Mr. B were engaged in a high-stakes poker game while Crusher looked on.

Tyrone eyed us with beef from the get-go. There was no love lost with Ty. He had feuded with Diamond a few years back over Tamara's affections. It's not that Tamara even paid Tyrone any mind; and it's not even like she and Diamond were official-official at the time. But it was generally understood that Tamara and D was, like, a thing, y'know?

Ty either didn't see it that way or didn't care. He'd pick Tamara up from school, showing up with flowers and candy and stuff.

Everyone in the hood acknowledged it as a violation. By right, anyone could have smacked Ty. By honor, it was Diamond's duty.

Of course, he tried to wimp out of it.

Of course, Gage had to push the little chick-a-dee out of his nest.

"That nigga is straight pushing up on your girl," I told him.

"So, what am I supposed to do?" He bitched. "Fight him?"

"Ya damned skippy, you gotta fight that nigga. Diamond, sometimes, I just don't be knowing about you."

"What does that mean?"

I knew I had him then; just had to reel him in.

See, Diamond's my boy from way back. He know things about me that no one else does. And he understands me like no one else. Ever since we was kids, he was the only one who did not write me off as an aberration to society.

So I egged Diamond on until he went to pick Tamara up from school one day. I don't know what happened, I wasn't there. Diamond wouldn't speak on it. Neither would Tamara.

All I know is that Ty rolled up into Tiny's that night unable to get his fist around a beer glass and black and blue poking from underneath his shades.

Since then, every time Ty's eyes fell on Diamond, his gaze said that he never forgot that ass whuppin'.

Fuck him, I thought, *we gon' see each other soon.* I just felt it in my bones.

Everyone was suited up, but Mr. B was Dapper Dannest cat at the table. Rolex watch. Ivory-tipped walking cane. Tailored Armani suit. Handmade Italian leather loafers. The finest silk tie you would ever want to see with a platinum clip and matching cufflinks. He even had a platinum watch chain hanging from his vest.

When it came to appearances, Mr. B always stood out from the crowd.

"What took you so long?" he asked, his voice crackling like stiff parchment, focusing on his cards. He didn't even look up at us.

"Man, some flatfoots tried to give us a speeding ticket," I joked. "They held us for a while, 'til we told them we was coming to see you. Then they escorted us over here. They let us play with the sirens and everything."

I had to at least *try* an' lighten the mood a little.

Mr. B stayed unamused. He fanned and unfanned his cards with one swift motion. Man, he was graceful, like a prehensile panther that could stand on his hind legs.

When he looked up and saw Diamond, his eyes went bright for a second, like high beams or a camera flash.

"Diamond, my man, the master of rap." It sounded like he was singing a song. "What say, brother?"

"I'm just doin' my thing, Mr. B. Striving for perfection, you know."

"You got a record deal yet?"

"Still working on it."

Diamond shuffled around a bit. He was always nervous around Mr. B. Ever since we were younger. Don't know why—Mr. B was the only way of making cheddar we had.

"You know what you are, Diamond?" asked Mr. B. "A fuckin' ghetto supastar. That's what you are. A ghetto supastar."

I couldn't tell what he meant by that. Mr.B had this way of speaking that danced between mockery and sincerity. I could never tell which was which.

"He's a fuckin' ghetto supastar," he repeated. "Am I right, Gage?"

"You the man Mr. B," I said. It seemed like the right thing to say at the time.

"Well, it's gonna be another twelve hours before you're right again for the day," Mr B chuckled.

The table laughed along behind him—but you could tell that only JT and Crusher truly got the joke. It's not as if he said anything funny in particular; it's not that anyone at the table was required to laugh at the old gangster's gibes. It just happened that way. Shit, I even gave a chuckle, but became enraged when Diamond later explained what Mr. B meant.

"Where's Skids?" Mr. B asked, his face turning back to the sculptured mask that creates nightmares.

"I'll get him," said Tin, darting from the table.

I never trusted Tin. Something about him threw me off. His eyes never stayed focused, they kinda darted all over the place. It's not so much that he didn't look you in the eye—with as many ex-cons as there were in the hood, we knew better than to make eye contact with one another. It may create a sense of connection to most, but on the other side of the wall, eyeballing was a high offense; a prelude to drama.

So it wasn't that Tin didn't look at you when he talked, it's that he looked everywhere and nowhere. He was either looking for or hiding something. I wasn't comfy with those options.

But Mr. B liked him and kept him around. He wasn't cut from the same cloth as the rest of us. Me, Crusher, and the rest, even Diamond—we had trouble written all over us in different languages. Tin looked like an accountant or something and stayed nervous; the kinda cat that jumps at his own shadow. He was the one we sent back to the scene of the crime. Even when the police saw him with us, they were prone to think we were kidnapping or extorting him.

He returned shakily with Skids, a thin-lipped cat with a slick conk. The skinny man handed Mr. B a medium-sized package wrapped in brown paper and tied with plain yarn.

Mr. B held the package tenderly before sliding it to me.

"Gage," he said, "when you drop this shit off, you tell those slanty-eyed motherfuckers that if I ever hear they've been buying from Teddy again, their little dicks will be swimming in a cup of wonton soup. Understand?"

We left Mr. B to his card game.

Chinatown is a small nation unto itself. The street signs, storefronts, billboards—everything is written in those stick figure–like markings. Colorful lights and ornaments string between buildings and over shop windows. Paper banners stretch over the street, looking like remnants from some New Year's celebration. The sidewalks teem with life: people loaded with plastic-wrapped and brown-bagged bundles looking like refugees in a mass exodus, children on bicycles circle everywhere, and, despite the language barrier, I can tell that the husbands and wives are haggling in Cantonese.

Everything smells of fish. Even at this late hour, stores are open with rows of cartons filled with raw seafood, herbs, and roots. In the restaurants, cooked duck and pork (at least, I hope it's duck and pork) hang from the metal racks in the windows.

Michael pulls the Bronco across the street from a small dry cleaners which looks closed for the night, if it ever opened at all.

"Yo, is this spot cool?" I ask.

Michael pulls his twin Lugers from a hidden

compartment between our seats. The black guns let off a cool, deadly glow.

"I'm cool," he says authoritatively. "We give 'em what they want, they give us what we want—couldn't be more simple. These punk-ass niggas don't want none."

I shift my holster from my back and let it rest on my right side.

When we get to the cleaners, Michael raps his knuckles on the thin window. Moments later, a small Cantonese man peeks out from behind the dingy shade behind the door. He opens the door and bows reverently.

"Ahh, Gage," he says in his heavy accent. "Mr. Cheng has been expecting you." He smiles and nods. "And who is your friend?"

"Hey Ling," Michael says with light, mocking courtesy. "This is Diamond."

"Diamond—a jewel of a name," the small man smiles.

He leads us dehind the counter, through racks of clothing and down a musty, dark staircase. Its ceiling is so low and narrow that it strikes feelings of claustrophobia. It seems like the perfect place for an ambush. We'd be trapped like rats in a one-lane maze.

In the basement, a single naked bulb swings from a chain. Once my eyes adjust to the dim light, I make out several ancient dry-cleaning steam boards and pressing machines situated randomly around the room. Beyond the small room, there's a door, slightly ajar, with a light in it. It breathes too ominously to be a simple storage cabinet.

There's an overweight Asian man in his sixties sitting at a plain metal table located in the middle of the room. I immediately recognize him as Lui Cheng.

Shit, when the small man at the door said, "Mr. Cheng," I was hoping that he was referring to another Mr. Cheng, like another Mr. Smith or Mr. Brown.

Mr. Cheng was a reputed gangster, whose resume made Mr. B seem like a nickel-and-dime hustler. To call Cheng notorious was like calling Satan a mean guy. Drugs, guns, prostitution, gambling—you name it, Cheng did it.

He was sweating profusely and wiping his head with a yellowed handkerchief. Behind him were two pony-tailed Asians wearing black suits and sunglasses. I've heard about Cheng's infamous Black Light—trained with the samurai of Bushido and equipped with silver six-shooters—but to see them in the flesh shivers my marrow.

A woman, whom I assume is Cheng's wife, is busy trying to look like she's cleaning around the filth-encrusted basement. She nods at us, seemingly out of obligation.

"Green tea?" Mr. Cheng asks, pouring himself a cup of the steaming brew.

"I don't drink," says Michael.

"And your friend?"

"I'll pass."

Cheng goes on about the merits of green tea, how it invigorates and merges the body, mind, and soul. "I drink it every day," he chuckles with self-control. "Brings the fire and the water together nicely." He sips. "Are you sure . . . ?" he motions toward me with the kettle.

"We're here to do business," Michael snaps. "Not to sample the Orient."

"Of course, of course," Cheng apologizes. "Ohh . . . you have something for me, of course?"

"Of course," Michael replies.

I look at Mrs. Cheng, sweeping about. When she sees me looking at her, she crosses her slanty eyes at me with a racist verve. *Fuck you too, bitch.*

She must be psychic, 'cause she twists her face into a grotesque contortion of flesh and muscle. She steals a look at the open door.

If I had time, I'd flip a coin. But I don't. I go with my gut.

"Mind if I smoke?" I ask Cheng.

"Of course, of course," Cheng nods. "No problem. Green tea?" he asks again.

I ignore Cheng's offer and turn to Michael. "Got a smoke?"

Michael shifts underneath his jacket, looking for a cigarette we both know isn't there.

"Never mind," I say. "I got one."

I pull the .380 from my side and thrust it into Cheng's pelvis underneath the table.

Michael's weapon comes out swiftly and lines at Mrs. Cheng's head.

"Guns, boys?" Cheng asks with exaggerated politeness. "Is this how Mr. B does business. Please, please—we are all brothers."

"What's behind that door?" I ask, eyeing him with intensity.

"Oh, that's just cleaning supplies," Cheng laughed. "Dry cleaning materials. Very expensive, we must keep stocked. Deliveries only come once a—"

"So, you won't mind if I bust a cap that way?" Michael pulls his second weapon from his waist, keeping the first one trained on Cheng's wife, who's staring him down. "They're not combustible are they?"

"Hyuen!" Cheng calls out, rattles orders in Cantonese.

A young boy, about seventeen, comes out with a silencer-equipped Uzi switching his target between Michael and me.

"Guns, Cheng?" Michael mocks. "We're all brothers."

Michael tries to make light of the situation, but we're in way over our heads. Still, no shots have been fired and even if any were, it would only be a minor discrepancy—shoot-outs are almost mandatory in these types of situations.

But the silencer on that Uzi brings a new level of tension. Cheng's known for his viciousness and his plethora of weapons, but not their technology. Whomever's supplying Mr. Cheng with that type of hardware is a wild card I'm not willing to deal with.

"Ahh, you have something for me?" Cheng asks calmly.

The Black Light don't move, like the guards at Buckingham Palace. They don't worry me, because from all the stories I've heard, they're more assassins than security. We wouldn't be able to stop them anyway; wouldn't see them coming.

Michael takes the .9 millimeter off of Mrs. Cheng and gives the smiling man the brown package.

Cheng drops a single key on the table.

"You do know where the Blue Locust Inn is," he smiles.

Fuck, I hated the waiting. I've always hated waiting. Still do. I was of half a mind to go back and take those fuckin' Chinks to meet Confucius.

Diamond was getting on my last one—he was rummaging through all of my tapes, switching the dial on the radio, all types of nervous activities. Fuck, I was nervous, too, but you didn't see me getting all fidgety and shit.

We had been waiting in the car for Jeannine and Keisha to call for what seemed to be hours. See, when Cheng dropped a key for a motel room on the table, I was shook. But I took it. I had to. Yeah, I may be the best shot since Billy the Kid and Diamond's a steady trigger, but no way could we fuck with Cheng's men.

I took the key, scooped back to the Barracuda, and got the girls to go up into the room. Diamond was bitching about sending the lambs to the slaughter, but fuck, I had to do what I had to do. I couldn't return to Mr. B empty handed. I gave the girls the key, told them to go to the room.

"We'll be right back," I said. "We going to get some chips and stuff."

I figured they'd call us soon enough, we'd go upstairs, retrieve what was waiting for us, and that would be that.

But we were waiting forever.

Just when I was about to lose it, the girls jumped into the backseat.

Jeannine threw a knapsack into the front of the ride.

"Damned, nigga," she said. "Why you ain't just tell me you wanted me to do a pickup?"

BLUE ANGEL
(12" VERSION)

This morning the scent of frying bacon is the only thing to smell in the kitchen. I turn the burner off, scrape the scrambled eggs from the pan onto the plate, sliding them next to two pieces of lightly browned toast. I stick my fork into the eggs—they're light and fluffy, but a bit runny. I sneak a taste—perfectly seasoned, if I do say so myself.

What's that burning? I turn back to the stove—damned, how'd I forget about the bacon? I quickly grab the pan's handle.

"Aww, fuck!"

Hot. Hot. Hot. My fingers are burned, coated in hot grease.

"You alright in there, baby?" Ma calls from her bedroom. I didn't mean to wake her up.

"No problem, Ma." Just toasted the fuck out of my hand. "I'll be right there."

I run water over my burn, pat the bacon dry with a paper towel, place the strips on the plate with the rest of the food, put the plate on a tray with a glass of orange juice.

"Here, Ma, I made you some breakfast," I say, opening the door to her bedroom.

"Why'd you do that, boy? I told you as soon as my head stops hurting, I'm gonna get up from here."

"Ma, it's twelve o'clock already, and you haven't eaten anything."

Ma struggles into a seated position in bed. She tries to play it off, but I see how hard it is for her to even get up. I put out the tray in front of her and prop her up with some pillows.

"See, Ma? The bacon's just the way you like it."

"Looks burnt to me," she says.

She's impressed with the meal but I can tell she doesn't want to admit it or make a fuss. Knowing Ma, she probably views this as lavish treatment.

"That's exactly how you like it," I smile.

"You must have me confused with somebody else," she giggles, and gently places her hand on mine. "You're a good boy, Diamond," she says.

Through my forming tears, I can see her ducts are putting in work also. It pisses me off to see her like this. Ma has always been fiercely independent; raised me by herself through good times and bad with a firm guiding hand and a kind word. But now she's laid up in bed, reluctantly relying on me to help her through the day—cooking meals, shopping, cleaning up the apartment.

This is no migraine—this is so far beyond that. I want her to go see a doctor, but we really can't afford one. And she really can't afford any more time off.

"Now, Ma, just eat your breakfast and I'll see you later, okay?"

"And where are you going?"

"I have to go see Tamara," I say. "She is my girl, after all."

"Mmm-hmm." She gives me a look out the side of her face.

I bend down and kiss her lightly on the forehead. She beams up at me and starts to eat.

I pull up in front of 186-06 40th Avenue, almost ashamed to sully the area's picturesque beauty with my presence. When I get to the door, I make a call on my cellular.

"Lewis residence."

"W'sup, love?"

"Oh." She pauses. Then finally, "Hi, Diamond."

"Can I come see you?"

"I don't know . . . Can you?"

I did mention that she's a smart ass, didn't I?

"Don't be like that," I say.

"Whatever." She hangs up the phone.

Tamara answers the door wearing gray cotton sweats and a white T-shirt. Still, her butternut skin has a soft glow all the girls in the Barracuda could never seem to get, no matter how much high-fashion gloss they threw on their backs, painted on their faces, or sprayed on their bodies. Tamara's high is natural and as intrinsic as THC is to a cannabis plant. Her thin, long braids dance on her smooth shoulders as she cocks her head to one side.

"Do I know you?" she asks with a coy anger. "You look familiar . . . Diamond, is it?"

She turns, leaving me in the doorway to follow her in. I take a deep breath, cross the threshold, and follow her upstairs to her room.

Even from the steps, the light, sweet fragrance of sandalwood washes the musty, pungent odors of the hood from my mental. The sun, coming in from the bay window facing east, bathes her room with a natural incandesence that makes everything seem to glow. I often wonder what it would be like to wake up in the room with the sun in my face and her in my arms.

She ignores me as she lights another stick of incense, letting its tip burn bright orange before fanning it out and its light tendrils begin to fill the room. I sit on her bed and grab the stuffed Bugs Bunny I had won for her at Great Adventures, holding it as if to say, *Look, it's me, Diamond. I got you this Teddy Bear, remember? You love me. As a matter of fact, you're crazy about me.*

No dice.

"Are you gonna have time to do my hair?" I ask, removing my baseball cap.

"You have got to be kidding," she says, looking at me in passing—moreover, through me—as she sits at her desk and reads from her anatomy text.

After about three minutes of the infernal silence, Tamara stares at me coldly.

"No visit, no phone call, no nothing," she says with a tough edge to her voice.

Damn the woman is sexy when she's mad.

"This shit has got to stop," she continues. "I deserve better than this Diamond."

"Tamara, things come up. Why can't you understand how I live my life?"

"That's as good as you can do—things come up?" she huffs, rests her head in her hand. "Why can't you understand that I need some attention, Diamond? I don't ask for much, just a little bit of your time. Just break me off a little something to show that, 'Yeah, Tamara, I care for you and I'm going to put actions behind my words.'" She's almost crying now. "I don't ask for much Diamond. I really don't. And if you can't give me that—just a little time—then I don't think you're ready for a relationship."

Oh man. I don't know what I'd do without Tamara. Yeah, I cheat on her and all, but she's what keeps me going. As fucked up as it sounds, just knowing that she's there for me allows me to do all the other shit I have to do.

"I'm sorry about last night," I apologize. "I was at the recording studio until four in the morning."

"Diamond please," she says. There's no holding back the tears now—they leak down her face like there are holes in her eyes. "Please, please, please, don't disrespect me like that."

"What are you talking about?" I ask angrily.

"I called the studio when I came home from school and Catherine said you left since eight o'clock."

Fuck.

"What the hell you do that for? I ain't down with that. I don't need no woman checking up on me like you're my motherfuckin' mother, okay. I already have one mother and she's doing a fine job. If you want someone to check up on, I suggest you go have your own fuckin' kids."

She's crying now. Actually crying.

"Listen," I say softly, "I told you: Things come up. You tell me that you don't want to hear about what I have to do to keep food on my fuckin' table and then you bitch about me not telling you. Which is it? Let me know 'cause I'm lost."

"This is not about that and you know it Diamond!" she cried.

I walk over to her and put my arms around her, hold her tighter than I can ever remember. Damned, it has been a long time. I've almost forgotten how soft she feels, how she just feels *right* in my arms.

"What you think, I have another girl?" I ask.

"Do you?"

"Yeah," I say. "Between putting together my demo and keeping money coming into my house, I hardly have enough time for you, but I somehow, someway, find a way to stretch more than twenty-four hours out of a day and have another girl."

"That's not funny," she says, wiping her tears.

"Love," I say, "please don't get into hounding me. Why do you think the first thing they do to a baby when it comes out of the womb is cut the umbilical cord, huh? Man's got to be set free!" I laugh. "Babies, God, even medical science know that a nigga got to be out. You keep fuckin' around and you gonna set evolution back a couple a' thousand years; have niggas swinging from trees and shit."

She giggles in spite of herself. And I feel her shoulder blades shake against my chest.

"You too much, Diamond St. James," she smiles. "I'm sorry, but when I don't hear from you I assume the worst. It's okay when you're here, but when you're not, I worry. I'm sorry baby."

She looks up at me.

"Yeah, you do need to get your hair done, though," she laughs.

I bend down and kiss her eyes, licking what remains of her tears with my tongue. I move slowly across her face, getting to her nose. I feel her whole body relax.

I stand her up and slip her sweats and underwear down over her soft brown hips in one smooth motion. We kiss all the way to the bed. After she unbuckles my jeans, they fall around my ankles. She pushes me onto the bed.

I'm surprised at how wet she is when she slides down on top of me. She smiles knowingly and kisses me on the lips. The kiss lasts for a second, ten, or a half hour—I can't tell.

I feel her moans through the trembles in her tongue as it laps around my mouth like a drugged snake. She's a contained sea of passion bobbing up and down, up and down, down and up, over me. Slowly at first, then faster, she moves, clockwise to counter-clockwise in a rhythm and science that unlocks my wild side.

I speak in tongues, giving praise to gods whose names have not been heard by human ears for centuries. I ask dieties for strength.

They answer.

I push inside her, getting wild, primal, visceral. I dig deeper, as if I could actually run back to the womb. With each thrust, my fears and insecurities crawl out of me like electric spiders.

Michael, Ma, Marshall—they're all so far away now. These movements are my life, my sole purpose.

I thrust deeper, gyrate harder. I feel like I can read her mind—her fears, hopes, and dreams. Does she feel the same? Can she tell how I really feel about her? My fear of losing her? Would she love me despite my dependency on her?

Don't want to think about that. I push in her wildly, like a caged wolverine, tearing at her. She matches my intensity with hot stares.

"It's okay baby," she says. "You don't have to worry."

Please Diamond, slow down. You're hurting me.

He's mindless now. Moving out of fear, more away from the world than into me. I didn't know so many Black men to be scared in this world.

He pushes harder and harder, running up into me.

I've seen what happens to the strong ones—how they were made weak, humiliated, castrated or chastised. I hear my mother's voice in between his grunts.

"The only thing you can and need to do for a

Black man is love him and respect him," she says. "He doesn't get those things anywhere else in this world. If you want to keep him, you better give him that love and respect."

I cry. Not for me, but for Diamond. For Diamond, who battles with his demons so hard that he wrestles them onto paper; for Diamond, who's scared to death as to what society has to offer; for Diamond, who the statistics said would be dead in another few years. I cry for Diamond because he would never cry for himself.

He begins to shake and quiver inside me, his motions becoming spastic and uneven. I can feel his every muscle cringing, tensing, and releasing seemingly hundreds of times per second. I feel the fire in his belly.

I sob, gasping and grabbing him tightly until there's nothing but my heaves and the gentle sounds of the trees outside.

"I don't know why I let you talk me into this, when I got to study," I say, though I don't regret a single moment.

"Like you didn't want to," he replies, kissing my forehead.

I kiss him full on the mouth, enveloping his satin lips.

He pulls back, gently holding my face in his hands, looking deeply into me. Aside from the occasional car that comes in a small escalating sound before returning into nothingness, there's pure silence. He lays with me, in me forever and ever.

*   *   *

Afterward, I braid his hair. It's like his sebaceous glands are portals to his soul. He opens up as I pull on his strands, telling me that his mother is sick and he thinks Michael is in trouble. He's worried about both of them. He tells me that Beemer is offering him some sort of opportunity, but it's still sketchy. "It's more extra-legal than illegal," he says.

It's times like this that remind me why I love Diamond. His world is so complicated and foreign to me, and I can feel the pressure he's under by the way his sentences trail off. He wouldn't be in so much trouble if he wasn't so noble, putting his dreams and the wants of others on an equal scale.

I still don't know about his rap dreams. I want him to have a skill that will help him make it in the real world. But when he talks about his music and future with such passion and belief, there's no way I can doubt that my baby is gonna be a star.

"Damn I've got class in a half an hour!" I realize when I'm done with the final cornrow.

"Don't sweat it baby," he says. "I'll drop you off."

Twenty-five minutes later, we pull up to the main building on campus. Some kids are hustling around, trying to get to class on time. Others languish on the lawn, reading quietly, talking in groups, or throwing Frisbees around.

I kiss him on the cheek and get out of the car.

"I'll see you later," he calls out the window.

"Okay," I say, knowing that it may be weeks before I see him again.

"You know," I say, "I don't see why you don't enroll for next semester. You're way smarter than most of the people in my class."

"Don't even go there," he says with a roll of his eyes.

"Alright," I back down. "Just a thought. I'll see you later, baby." I blow him a kiss and hurry off to class.

Tamara's always pushing school on me. I can't be mad, though, she's only doing what she feels best.

What would my life be like if I were to enroll in school? If I were to somehow find the funds and fortitude to walk down those halls of higher learning? I'd have a whole different gang of friends, that's for sure. Instead of packing guns, I'd be packing bookbags. Maybe I could study law and medicine, instead of being involved in street justice and drugs.

Look around at all of these preppy-looking motherfuckers, laughing as if they don't have a care in the world. Comparatively, they don't. They have all the advantages—educated and connected they'll probably get jobs right out of college, joining the rat race, living in the 'burbs with their happy little families.

My cell phone rings, snapping me out of my dreamscape.

"Speak."

"It's Gage, nigga."

"Oh, what up, son?"

"Where you at? We gotta finish last night's job. Meet me at the crib."

"A-ight. Gimme like twenny minutes."

"Out." He hangs up the phone.

I take one last look at the sea of students milling about. They look so happy, full of direction and potential—not. They're all schmucks. Fuck 'em.

DIRTY CASH
(MAKE MONEY REMIX)

We roll up to the Red Pussy, a low-maintenance strip club in Flatbush, a little after three o'clock. At the bar, I order a Godfather, chilled, with no ice. The barkeep puts in way too much scotch.

On a beat-up stage decorated with Christmas lights (about a third of which are not working), a lone stripper, a tired-looking woman in her forties, grinds awkwardly to a Rick James tune that I used to know the words to. Surprisingly agile for her age, she does a syncopated slink, peeling off her torn fishnets before throwing them over her shoulder onto the table of a leering geezer.

I think about Ma, working long nights to help keep my belly full, and find deep wells of pride and virtue in the woman's off-beat movements. I guess what people do for money may be secondary to why they do it.

The archaic stripper tells me a few things with her smile before fingering me over. Whether out of pity or curiosity, I comply.

"Hey sugar," she jabs one bony hip my way. "How 'bout a fiver for momma?"

"C'mon," says Michael, motioning me to the back of the club with his head. Standing in front of the kitchen's swinging doors is a dark, bald brother with a bushy goatee.

To call the room a kitchen is a bit flattering. As far as food-preparation appliances, there are two deep fryers, a double sink, and a microwave. In one corner are metal shelves stocked with pretzels, peanuts, and chips. Next to it is a large freezer. There's a small door marked TOILET.

The bald man opens the door to the bathroom. It's small, just a commode, sink, and a mirror, and stinks of day-old urine and vomit. Baldy knocks three times on the wall behind the bowl.

Seconds later, the dirty wall panel slides open. We maneuver around the toilet into another room.

The first thing I see is the money. Heaps of it; large bills with big faces spread out on a huge mahogany table. It's more than I've ever seen at one time, save for a few PBS specials on counterfeiting or the U.S. mint. About eight sketchy individuals sit around the table. They're uneasy and eager, but obviously happy to see us.

A sneaky-looking brother with Jheri curls and a gold tooth waves Michael over.

Michael walks over to the table, surveying the pile of dead presidents, and hands the backpack to the Eazy-E-looking cat. The man checks the bag, making sure the locks on the zippers haven't been tampered with. Satisfied, he hands over a rubber-banded knot of hundred dollar bills. We're whisked out of the room without a word.

Once we make it back to Tiny's, Michael heads straight to Mr. B's office. I'm finishing a watered-down Long Island iced tea when Michael takes the stool next to mine.

"My man," he smiles, slapping a fat roll of twenties into my palm. There has to be at least five hundred dollars in it.

"What's this?" I ask.

"Mr. B's just showing a little extra appreciation for the fine work we been doing for him."

I pocket the wad without counting it.

"We keep this going and you'll have enough money to make your own album," Michael smiles.

"We keep this going and all we gonna make is the six o'clock news or the obituary columns."

He glances at me sideways. "What's this—you goin' soft bro?"

"Naw, man, I just want to live. That's all."

"Well, you need money to live. Right now, we barely surviving."

"Yeah, and fuckin' around with you got me nearly dyin'. What the fuck was that shit last night all about?"

"Son, son," he says. "You know I got your back."

"Don't give me that shit. I had a fuckin' Uzi in my grill. That shit ain't cool."

He's silent for a moment. "D, I'ma be straight with you, yo. I don't know what the fuck is going on. But then again I do."

He pauses for a moment, then orders a beer.

"You ever heard of Little John?" he asks, sipping on the frosted green bottle.

"Ain't that one of Robin Hood's merry men?"

He laughs. "Man, you closer to the truth than you know." Another sip of beer.

"There's these cats from North Carolina—they called the Robbing Hoods," he says, serious once more. "They part of the reason why Mr. B hasn't been able to expand—they hate his ass."

"And what else is new?" I ask. "Everyone hates Mr. B."

"Yo, you remember like two years ago, when I *stayed* paid?" he asks.

Of course I remember. Two years ago, Michael's money seemed never ending. His pockets weren't just deep—they were bottomless. That's when he purchased the Bronco. He'd take me to all types of big-dollar parties, buying the most expensive liquors and fine cuisine.

"You ain't never asked yourself why that shit stopped?"

"I know that the game has its rainy seasons and its dry spells," I say. "I just figured shit went away."

"Yeah, well the river had dried up big time. See, I used to go down South, packs of cocaine taped to my underarms. Man, that shit was the worst. The dogs would come around—I used to be shitting cinder blocks, son. For real.

"Anyway," he continues, "Little John and the Hoods stuck me up one time. Put fuckin' M-16s to my temple." His eyes glassed over as he sipped his beer and dazed off into the mirror. "They told me to tell Mr. B that he wasn't welcome south of Jersey."

He sips his beer and lets it wash around in his mouth before swallowing. "We had to lay low for a minute, tuck our hands in our pockets. Mr. B didn't want to get into it with those cats—it would be too much trouble to send the amount of arms down there that we would need to handle them.

"Well, two months ago, Little John wound up missing. Three weeks ago, he wound up found. He was with his car in the back of an eighteen-wheeler in an old parking lot. Apparently, John got hijacked and was left in the truck's cargo bay to die slowly. They said the smell jumped out of the truck like a backdraft when they opened it up."

We finish our drinks in silence.

Michael's mood stays somber as we drive back to his house to pick up my Cutlass. That is, until we see Hollis walking down the street.

"Just look at that brother, man," Michael says, scoping the dealer real hard. "He literally holds the key to our future on his wrists, on his finger, and in his pockets."

"You don't ever ease up, do you?"

He grins devilishly. "That's cool, D. Just think about it alright?"

BLUE ANGEL
(TOUCH ME IN THE
MORNING REMIX)

The apartment is dark when I get home.

"Ma?"

No answer.

Her bedroom door is half open. She must be sleeping.

I peek into the room. No sign of her. The pillows from this morning are still propped up, the plate of food on the bed, half eaten.

I make it to the kitchen with quick steps.

There she is, lying face down on the linoleum tile. The telephone is off the hook, its receiver dangling by its cord just inches from her hand.

Jesus Christ! "Ma!" *Damnedwhatthefuckohshittohigh hellJesusChrist.*

"MA!"

I run over and grab her in my arms. Thank God—she's still alive, her eyelids fluttering, her breath ragged and faint.

I grab the phone, dial 9-1-1, cradle her head against my chest. After an eternity, an operator comes on the line.

"This is 9-1-1. What is your emergency?"

"My mom passed out and she needs an ambulance, bad!"

"Where are you located?"

I give her the address, which opens the doorway to a room of inane questions. "Was your mother shot or stabbed?"

"No."

"Is she still breathing?"

"Just barely. She looks real bad. She's all shaky and her eyes are very puffy. Just get someone here fast, okay?"

"Sir, the ambulance is already on its way. What is your name, sir?"

"Diamond St. James."

"Diamond, was this a break and entry, or any sort of domestic dispute?"

"No."

"Was there any foul play involved?"

"No she's sick. What the fuck can you not understand?!"

"Okay, Diamond, but we have to know what's going on. Is this in any way related to drugs, prescription or otherwise?"

"No bitch, I just came home and found her passed the fuck out!"

The operator was silent for a moment. "So you said she's not on any medication."

"Fuck you bitch!!" I scream. "Just get a fuckin' ambulance over here. Now, Goddammit!"

I hang up the phone, draw Ma so close to me, I feel her heart rate. It's beating about a million times a second. "Just hold on, Ma," I say, stroking her hair. "You're gonna be alright."

After five minutes, her breathing is so shallow that I can barely feel it when I put my ear to her nose.

"Please don't die on me, Ma. Please don't die. You gotta stay strong, okay Ma? An ambulance is coming, just hang in there."

Three minutes later, I take her down three flights of steps and lay her across the loveseat in the Cutlass.

At the corner, I see the EMS truck. I jerk my car's nose in front of them, cutting them off.

"She's in the backseat," I shout, jumping out of my ride.

A fat man with a thick mustache and an EMS cap walks over to the backseat. Ma's eyes are rolled back into her head so all you could see was white pearls in her sockets.

The EMS worker reaches down to check her vital signs.

He shakes his head and tells me that she's gone.

INTERLUDE

I sit with Diamond in the Reverend Snider's office. He hasn't let go of my hand since this morning.

The reverend rests back, crossing his hands over his ample belly. "As I was explaining, Diamond, Rosehill is quite a popular cemetery—you can agree as to its beauty, I'm sure. We're one of the few Baptist parishes in Brooklyn that offers such a wide range of funeral and burial services, so our spaces are usually reserved years in advance. But, because your mother was a dedicated member of our congregation, we will make room for her—we do keep some plots reserved for such instances."

"Still," he says leaning on his desk, "there are the monetary considerations."

He thumbs through the thick catalog of coffins before him with self-serving smugness.

"Reverend Snider," Diamond says, "you're asking for three thousand dollars. I just don't have that type of money."

"Unfortunately, we're not in the business of

providing free plots. Now, we have some payment plans," he says, moving to the back of the catalog.

"So what you're telling me is that she can't be buried in her own church's cemetery."

I grab his hand tighter. He's been through a lot in the past twenty-four hours. I can only imagine how hard it's been for him not to take his pain out on the world. I'm surprised he hasn't lashed out at someone already—he's always misdirected his anger. Still, I wouldn't blame him if he let this pompous hypocrite have it.

"The cemetery used to belong to the church, but it's under the management of Brown's Funeral Home Association," says the reverend. "We just aren't allowed to make special deals."

"Well, can't you talk to the funeral home, explain that my mother was a faithful and dues-paying member? I mean, isn't Deacon Brown on the board of directors? That must count for something."

Please Diamond, don't beg. Don't give him the pleasure.

"Why, yes and no. You see, the deacon keeps his private business practices divorced from his ecumenical role. We have to do that, it's only ethical. That way, the same rules apply to members and nonmembers alike. There is really nothing I can do about it."

"Look, Reverend, my mother worked fourteen hours a day, six days a week. She didn't make a lot of money, but still, every Sunday she tithed; put ten percent of her wages in your collection plate."

"She was a good and faithful servant," the Reverend Snider says. "I know the Lord has a special place for her in Heaven."

"You can keep all those mansions in the sky. I just want to give my mom a decent burial, that's all."

"I understand Diamond, but it's really out of my hands."

Humph. Sounds like Pontius Pilate turning over the Messiah.

"Like I said, there are some payment options, if you look just back here—"

"Can't you take up a special collection for her or something?" I interrupt.

He throws me a patronizing smile, then rubs his chin and looks as if we're wasting his time. "I wish I could, but, you see, uhh, Tamara is it? We just had a special offering this past Sunday to pay for our new organ. I don't think it would be fair to the congregation to ask them for more."

He pauses as if deep in thought, shakes his head, then seems inspired.

"I tell you what I'll do for the two of you, and for your mother of course." He circles one finger in the air. "I usually charge a fee of six hundred dollars to perform the funeral services. For you though, I won't charge anything. It's the best I can do. Now that would bring your total cost down to . . . Let me see here . . ."

He punches numbers into his calculator.

Diamond surprises me with how fast he leaps out of his chair.

"You charge people for being dead, too?" he

asks, viciously. I've never heard him sound like *this* before.

The man of God remains silent.

"So that's how it is, huh? The church is in the business of being in business."

The Reverend Snider lets out a deep sigh as if to show his understanding of our situation. Maybe the Devil is fooled, but no one in this room is. We walk out in silence.

"What are we going to do?" I ask Diamond, once we're in the car.

"This is my problem," he says. "And I'm going to take care of it my way."

Lord, help us all.

MURDER THEM

As the choir's precentor and a lifelong member of the parish, Shirley had a set of eyes privy to many of Rosehill Baptist Church's great mysteries. She saw the reverend comforting many of the congregation's young widows, selflessly counseling them in his private room in the rectory at all times of night. She saw Deacon Brown, blessed as he was, tend to a young child every other weekend— and the love the child had for the deacon, gleaming wildly every time he saw the clergyman.

But such sacrifices were necessary in order to serve the Lord. They would go to great lengths to protect the privacy of these ladies, even having the occasional church member, who would see them before or after the private ablutions, swear to secrecy. "These young ladies already have so many eyes upon them because of their, ahh, predicaments," the clerics would say. "We wouldn't want them embarrassed by receiving special aid from the church—you do understand?" Still, none of this knowledge was as telling as the church's "other" bank account, where the ministers kept the root of all evil safely tucked away from the church members. For surely had the congregation been informed of the plumpness of Rosehill Baptist Church's coffers, they would feel less obligated to tithe weekly. And even a heathen knows how important financial contributions are to the chur—err, ahh, God.

So, of course, Shirley had never feasted her eyes on such a heretic sight as when she looked up to throw her devotions to the man above and saw the masked boys coming up the aisle, brandishing weapons with blasphemous audacity.

They moved among the flock as if protected from detection by the forces of the netherworld. They were halfway up the temple, but the air left Shirley too quickly for her to speak anything of value. She made the sign of the cross and maundered a litany of holy names.

The congregation, heads bowed, genuflected in their pews as they followed the Reverend Snider in prayer. A steady rolling of low, reverent voices vibrated off the stained-glass windows, chandeliers, and silk bouquets of roses. Then all heaven and hell broke loose.

It was the Reverend Snider, obviously forgetting his place, who snapped the church to attention with a rendition of the Immaculate Conception.

"Holy fuck!"

The gun's twin barrels of the one with the John Wayne mask got a bead on the clergyman.

The other, looking like William Shatner, turned

to face the entrance and panned a .45 automatic over the frightened mass.

Some grasped rosaries; others mumbled inaudible devotions.

The church became purgatory, neatly tucked in a forgotten fold of time's fabric. There was a non-silence; at once, bliss and void: The hum of the oscillating fans churned the chorale of seraphs and cherubs accompanying the congregation through their darkest hour, or, maybe, they were already in Abraham's bosom and it was an elegy from those they left behind. Their breaths were the sounds of clouds parting for the return of the First Cause, or, perhaps, the ripping of the earth as the Prince of Darkness drew first blood at Armageddon. The roaring truck outside was the stone being rolled back from Christ's tomb on the third day, but then again, it may have just been the Lord of Darkness's long tail dragging over Calvary . . . as he marched down the aisle.

One woman passed out.

Then another . . . and another.

And another. Four in total.

A few men bit their lips, wishing those young punks were just a bit closer. The children seemed immune to it all . . . if their parents were scared enough after this incident, perhaps they'd be allowed to sleep in on Sundays.

The Reverend Snider thought he recognized the eyes peering through the false face behind the two handguns, but banished the notion. The gunman in front of him was crazy as the demon-possessed man from Gerasenes, and, unless the Messiah planned on making an impromptu visit to East New York, there would be no way to cast his legion into the swine.

"What a gwan, Duke?" the Starfleet commander asked behind him, doing his best Rasta-man imitation.

The other's laugh was as comforting as a fingernail scratching across a blackboard. He ran to the chancel, his weapons trained on the reverend.

The man of the cloth got to his knees and begged.

He was swiftly kicked in the belly.

"Sing some shit!" the boy commanded the choir.

"I have seen the coming of the glory of the Lord . . ." Shirley began. The choir and the organ player quickly fell in step.

The assaulter waved his Nines about like a double-batoned conductor.

The fake Jamaican scudded to the front of the church and grabbed the collection baskets. He had never seen them empty. Their depth was amazing.

"In a short while," John Wayne said as he moved behind the lectern, "the good captain will be coming around and taking a special collection for a worthy cause. As he makes his rounds, we expect each and every one of you God-fearing people to do the right thing. Please, give generously."

He secured one of the guns behind his belt buckle, peered over the crowd, then began thumbing through the Good Book before him.

"That's enough," he said after a while, waving the exposed gun over the choir.

The nonsilence returned.

"We will be reading today from the Book of Proverbs, chapter eleven. 'The Lord abhors dishonest scales, but accurate weights are his delights.' Is there anyone here who does not have his scales balanced?" he asked. " 'When pride comes, then comes disgrace, but with humility comes wisdom.' Anyone here too proud?"

James T. Kirk handed the first basket to a frightened lady in the front row. He made sure that everyone filled it with money, jewelry, and watches—everything except wedding bands—before emptying the coffer's contents into a large garbage bag.

The Reverend Snider, always placing the needs of others before his, crawled toward the rectory door. He was, of course, making his escape. To go away. To call the police, that is. But not from the church, he thought. That would be too dangerous. Down the block. From a pay phone. Or maybe a few blocks farther, where he could be sure he wasn't followed. Yes, he could catch a cab and bring the police back himself. After all, were the police to come in from his phone call, they would come in like rogues, shotguns drawn, adorned in riot gear, with no regard for the Lord or human life. So it was decided: The only righteous thing to do was get in a cab and not come back with the police until he was sure that the gunmen had fled and that the situation was safe.

John Wayne thumbed through the Good Book again. "Deuteronomy, chapter one, verse nine: 'At that time I said to you, "You are too heavy a burden for me to carry alone. The Lord your God has increased your numbers so that today you are as many as the stars in the sky. May the Lord, the God of your fathers, increase you a thousand times and bless you as He has promised! But how can I bear your problems and your burdens and your disputes all by myself? Choose some wise, understanding and respected men from each of your tribes, and I will set them over you.' "

Kirk passed a large man, who emptied his pockets of change and a few bills, then sat back, folding his hands over his chest.

"Star, me know you have more than dat pon you." He pointed his gun at the man's bulky breast pocket.

The man slowly pulled out a pregnant wallet and placed it in the basket with the rest of the loot.

The de facto church leader continued: "Do not show partiality in judging; hear both small and great alike. Do not be afraid of any man, for judgment belongs to God. Bring me any case too hard for you, and I will hear it."

Now! the Reverend Snider thought.

He dashed for the door. But his knees were not as responsive as they used to be. The boy at the altar grabbed him by his vestments, placed the gun in his mouth. The cold barrel scratched his tonsils.

"Man, I ought to blow your fuckin' head off right here."

A glare of recognition in the clergyman's eyes.

"Do you know what it means to hear Ezekiel 25:17 in this situation?" he asked the terrified man.

An elderly woman placed her wooden cane between her legs, shifted through her purse for a donation.

"Easy princess," the boy said softly. "Keep your coin."

"No, no, no," she contested. "I'll do whatever I can to cast out the demons that have driven you boys here today." She placed a few crumpled bills and food stamps in the basket. "It is never too late for penitence. The Lord will forgive you."

The young man with the Captain Kirk mask paused. The large man, the cheap one who had given him problems, lunged at him clumsily. It had seemed much easier in his mind. He had meant to hold the youth in a headlock, but was one second too slow and only grabbed the villain about the waist.

The boy repeatedly beat down on the man's head with the Remington's butt until blood began to spurt. The man passed out.

He heard a gunshot behind him.

Nonsilence.

The Black Talon ricocheted and echoed through the church.

More nonsilence.

The brass cartridge clanged and rolled across the marble floor.

Diamond turned to see the Reverend Snider

sprawled out behind the pulpit, his body twitching as his soul ascended to New Jerusalem.

Gage stood up with blood on his hands.

"What the fuck is taking so long?" He pointed his guns toward either side of the church. "Now let's move it!"

AMAZING GRACE
(PART 1)

It's one of those mornings when the sky cries so much that she washes off her blue skin and turns gray; where the clouds frown and the sun hides, ashamed and scared to peer downward. The birds fly about aimlessly—no patterns, no purpose. The trees shuffle in confusion like my ancestors first getting off of slave ships.

"Ashes to ashes, dust to dust . . ."

Several mourners huddle around the open grave as Rose St. James's coffin is lowered into the ground. There are a few members of the congregation—I guess that's who they are. I recognize Rose's nephew Malik in the wheelchair.

Of course, I know Diamond. I would know him anywhere.

He's not in this world. He seems deaf to the minister's prayers, staring coldly as the coffin disappears from view. The girl next to him is beautiful, so much like Rose twenty years ago—vulnerable but not weak, defiant but not stubborn. Wholesome. Good. Attracted to trouble.

She cries soft tears, the type that burn away fear.

The boy on Diamond's side seems like someone with God in his heart but the Devil in his mind. He can only be Diamond's best friend.

Diamond steps forward and throws a handful of dirt onto the coffin.

Ashes to ashes, dust to dust.

He turns. He sees me, stares directly into my soul—he's unsettled. He knows, but he doesn't *know*.

He studies my features but doesn't want to believe the truth.

His girlfriend is confused; his best friend ready to fight.

An intense chill runs up my spine like a rabid mongoose. I'm looking through a time-refracted mirror. When he sees my wedding band, he stops denying what he's known since he saw me.

"I'm sorry about your mom," I say.

He's silent, looking for answers to questions he doesn't know how to ask.

"What are you doing here?" he finally asks.

"If you don't want me here I'll leave," I say. "But I had to come."

"Why?" He stabs me with his eyes. "You weren't here for her when she was alive. And I know you sure ain't come for me. So what is it?"

I almost want to laugh. He is my son, inside and out. I can almost tell him what he'll say next, pull the words from his brain. But I expected as much——the pain, the anger, the resentment.

"I'm sorry," I offer, though I know he won't accept it. "That's all I can say."

I turn and walk away. He's not ready for me yet.

There he is, walking away—my motherfuckin' sperm donor, walking out of my life. Again. Why here? Why today? Of all times. That self-serving bastard. Couldn't he have just hid in the shadows or something? Why did he show himself? Does he want to talk? To reconcile? What does he really want? What do I say to him?

He's a good fifty feet away when I decide to run after him.

I know he hears me. Why doesn't he turn around?

I come around. We stand face to face.

"What kind of game are you getting, materializing here like some ghost from a fog, when you haven't been around for the past seventeen years? You gotta tell me something, man."

"I had to pay my last respects," he says. "And, whether you believe this or not, Diamond, I wanted to see you. I didn't expect you to greet me with open arms, but I had to make sure you were alright; that you were handling everything fine. I'm making myself available because I don't feel you should be alone at this time."

"Well, I'm not alone."

He looks over my shoulder to Michael and Tamara, and nods knowingly.

"I guess I shouldn't have come then."

"So that's it? You say your piece and turn your back on me again?"

"What do you want me to say? That there's no excuse for me walking out on you and your mom? That what I did was wrong? I can't give you those clichéd answers just now, Diamond. This is not the setting for that discussion."

I hear him. I hear the earth turning, feel my heart lump in my throat.

"So am I gonna see you again, or is this it?"

"Would you trust my answer?" he asks. Then, "There's no place I have to be. I was planning on staying for a little while. I'd really like to spend some time with you. It's long overdue. And something like this just makes me realize how much time we don't have."

A shrug of my shoulders is all I can muster, I still don't know whether to smack him or hug him, or both, or in which order. Fuck, he's the closest family I got now.

But he made his decision a long time ago. Now I make mine.

"See you around," I say, and rejoin the people who truly care about me.

"I still can't believe your old man showed up like that—that's so fuckin' hot, son," Michael is saying in the backseat of the Cutlass about a half hour later as he, Tamara, and I drive home. "He's checking for you, D—don't spit on that. Only a father can raise a man. I think you should hear him out."

"If Diamond doesn't want to see his father, what is it to you?" Tamara says. "Don't you think there's enough going on already?"

"Bitch, I wasn't talking to you."

What the fuck?!

No way, not today.

I stomp on the brake pedal and the car stops violently, everyone jerks forward.

"Come on," I say, opening up the back door to let Michael out. "Come on."

"What the fuck is going on here?" Michael asks surprised.

I grab him by his lapels and pull him onto the sidewalk.

"Nigga, is you crazy?" he screams.

We stand toe to toe.

"Did you just call my girl a bitch?" I ask. I clutch my fists, not to intimidate him, but to hold back from wailing on him. Every muscle in my body is afire. *I'm ready to give it all to you, Michael. You can take it all off my shoulders right here and now. Just say the word.*

"Yo, D, chill," he looks for a forgiveness that doesn't live here anymore. "It's me, Gage. Son, are you okay?"

I say nothing; which says more than words ever could right now.

"Oh man, son. You want to take it to the square over a bi——I mean girl? C'mon, man."

Silence.

"Apologize," I say.

"What?"

"You heard me nigga, apologize."

"Alright, alright. Yo, D, I'm sorry, man. I ain't know you was—"

"Not to me." I motion my head toward the car. "To her."

"Awww, man. Why you buggin'?" He whines, looks at me.

Please call this a bluff, nigga. Please.

He twists up his nose and walks over to the car. We drive the rest of the way in silence.

GHETTO SUPASTAR

A ghetto may be a ghetto, but Uptown is a different animal, with mores, customs, and traditions as distinct from Brooklyn as a cheetah is from a leopard. Diamond walked around in circles through throngs of shirtless teens, Latinos, and single mothers. Everything was so different. People's actions, greetings, interactions—they all seemed new. The winos and drug addicts had a flair built out of this hovel. If you were to peel back the layers of their uncleansed skin, you could read Uptown's history just as a scientist uses layers of earth to puzzle together the past.

It was the perfect place for him to be. He needed an escape from his reality, but not reality itself. He couldn't stand to be inside of anything, not even his skin.

On some block, somewhere—hadn't he passed here three times already?—he saw a crude omen resting by the base of a tree. It was an offering to some unknown god, a box of broken coconut shells filled with beans. There were also animal

144

parts that baked in the heat of the night, their stench sticking to the air on a molecular level. Next to the box was an old can of coffee grinds that was filled to the rim with what looked like animal fat suspended in cooking oil.

"Are you finished with that drink?" a woman asked. She was wearing a short blue denim dress and old tennis sneakers that showed her ashy ankles. Her hair was short, not cut short, but short as if her follicles were, by some ungodly mandate, allowed to push out only but so much hair in between her bald patches. Her face was marked up with bruises, her lips full and black.

Diamond looked at his bottle of beer, which was half full, and handed it to the woman. He couldn't drink anymore with the putrid odor of the beans, shell, and *what kind of liquid was that?* flaming his nostrils anyway.

She thirstily gulped it down.

"Ummmm," she smiled, and when she spoke her plump tongue came through her missing teeth. "Still cold."

This really is a different part of town, he thought.

"Thanks," she said, swaying giddily. "You don't know how long I been wanting a drink." She slinked closer to the generous boy.

"Where are you going?"

"Just walking," he said.

"Hmmm. You too young to be fooling around, ain't you?"

"C'mon." Diamond protested. "Too young for what?"

145

She came closer still and looked down at his pants.

"What you got down there?" she asked, her eyes going from his and down to his crotch. "Ooh, you got a lot of you down there."

By all measures he should have been repulsed by this woman.

He wasn't. He felt himself rising beneath his jeans.

There was a sensuality about her voice, an intoxicating suggestiveness to her movements he couldn't deny. In spite of himself, he was attracted to her.

"So what you got?" she repeated, looking around.

"What *you* got?" he asked back slyly, as if he were wooing her. He found it almost impossible not to talk to her like she was the most beautiful woman he had ever seen.

"I got me," she said.

"How much is you?"

"Ten dollars."

"Ten dollars? C'mon, I just gave you some beer."

"You got seven?"

He had seven.

She stroked his pants, grabbing the stiffening part in her hand. "You from around here?"

"Yeah," he lied. "Right around the corner."

"Where's around the corner?"

"Right there on Edgecombe." Diamond had not realized that he was still on Edgecombe Avenue,

146

that the street had just taken a swift turn. This alarmed the woman.

"You not 5-0 are you?" she asked.

He giggled off her insinuation.

"Gotta ask," she apologized. "You got a condom?"

"I just want my dick sucked," he said plainly.

"Oh, you gonna get you some nice deep throat, boo."

She walked over to some benches that lined the sidewalk and made her way over the small side of a large boulder. She looked like some sort of impoverished guide, leading him into uncharted wilderness. He followed her casually. By the time Diamond got over the boulder she was several feet ahead making her way to a clearing littered with condoms, cigarette butts, and bloodied underwear.

She sat down on a rock. "Right here, boo."

She stroke him again. "Oh you large," she complimented, tapping twice on his zipper. "You know you gotta open up."

Her voice was sensual and inviting. There was a certain suggestiveness to her speech—abrupt, direct, and open—which he couldn't deny. Her cadence was like miniature suites in an opera, tapping into the carnal closet of his mind.

He unzipped and his penis pointed out at her like a divining rod.

"Money," she said real business-like, rubbing her fingers together, yet never taking her eyes off of what was in front of her. He handed her a crumple of bills.

"That's seven, right?" she asked.

"Five," he said.

"Oh, boo—why you trying to play me?" she teased.

"Alright," she said after a slight pause. " 'Cause you gave me a beer."

She counted the money and went straight to work, covering him whole with her full lips. Her fingers ran his length, building his arousal steadily.

"You almost there, boo," she said, looking up at him.

She went back to work. Soon enough, Diamond felt a stream emptying from him. She quickly backed off and spit to the ground, then got up and walked away. After a few steps, she turned to him.

"That was good, right?"

"Yeah," he surprised himself with his own delight. "You work over here?"

"Why?" she flirted. "You wanna see me again?"

"Yeah."

"When you wanna see me?"

"Later. About twelve."

"Twelve o'clock?" she asked as if she had to check her schedule. "I'll be at the hotel on the corner."

"You work there?"

She laughed. "I live there."

She looked him up and down in a way that made him feel sexy, worth something.

"My name is Shawn," she said walking away. "I'ma be waiting out there. And don't be coming with all your friends and blowing up my spot."

She lifted up her skirt as she walked, leaving Diamond with a vision of flabby, onyx buttocks.

A few seconds later, a beer-bellied man with a baseball cap and a beard came creeping out of the bushes. He followed Diamond out.

He figured him to be Shawn's pimp.

He was two blocks away when he noticed a beat cop eyeing him knowingly.

Diamond didn't know what to think. He'd been through so much, done so much, seen so much in the past week, that he knew he was under arrest for something. It didn't matter what it was—he was sure that he was guilty. It was a long time coming, and he knew the rules—he wouldn't turn on Michael or Mr. B for all the amnesty in the world.

"Hey," the cop called, moving closer with a smile. "What's up?"

Diamond just looked at him. He knew the tricks, the traps, and the runnings. His mouth stayed shut.

The officer grinned widely. "You don't remember me, do you?"

Diamond peered underneath the man's cap.

" 'St. James—no Walkman's in the hall,' " he bellowed with a laugh.

Diamond smiled. It was Nixon—he used to be a security guard when Diamond was in high school.

"What's up man?" Nixon smiled. "What you been up to? How's the rapping thing? I hear you're still doing it."

"Yeah, yeah, no doubt," Diamond said anxiously. He was never more than passing acquaintances with the man when he was in school, and now, even in parts removed from his home turf, he did not want to be seen cavorting with police.

"You ever thought about getting down with the force?" Nixon asked with a recruiting smile. "It pays pretty well. You know," he said with secrecy, "we need more brothers in blue."

"Yeah," Diamond said. He needed to get the conversation over with as soon as possible.

"I'm fresh out the academy," beamed Nixon, proudly. "They'll be testing again in a few weeks. You don't want to miss it."

"Yeah, yeah."

"All you have to do is go down to a precinct and pick up an application—you have your diploma, right?"

"Nah," Diamond lied, hoping it would deter the man and send him on his way.

"Well, you gotta get your G.E.D., brother," Nixon advised. "And Sanitation is testing next Tuesday. It may be too late for that one—but my sister works there, she could help you out if you really want it. Let me get your number and I'll call you with all the info."

Diamond rattled off any seven numbers. The cop asked him to repeat the numbers four different ways, obviously part of his training to discern when those damned detainees were trying to pull a fast one. Had he not so much practice memorizing his rhymes he would have faltered.

"Alright, brother," Nixon said, slapping palms with the boy off beat, proud that he was able to merge his academy training, street savvy, and inside connects to the hood in one triumphant moment of community policing. He would run a search on the boy when he got back to the station house that night. Hell, he'd make sergeant sooner than anyone thought.

When Diamond got back to Malik's crib, his cousin was in the living room playing with his two-year-old daughter, Siyana, who was running around wearing nothing but a diaper and a T-shirt. It was a wonder how Malik could maneuver his wheelchair through the clutter, much less take care of an overenergized baby girl.

"Damned, where you been all this time?" Malik asked.

"Walking."

"I feel you," Malik said. "Losing Aunt Rosie has been hard for me, too. Just watching Dad go through it has been terrible. He couldn't even bring himself to come to the funeral. He refuses to believe that his little sister is gone. I figure it's gonna take some time."

"Yeah," Diamond said, but he really wasn't listening. He went into the bedroom and crashed out.

His dreams were vicious.

It was all there: the collection basket, the Reverend Snider, and John Wayne. Diamond wrestled with the large man who in tonight's dream looked like his father, or the brother he never had, then Mr. Williams, his fifth-grade English teacher, then Nixon the cop.

There was the marriage of flesh and lead, ending in a divorce of blood and bone. Then that eerie silence in which the shell dropped in stereo sound with reverbs. And then the baby crying.

Diamond looked at the altar. John Wayne was on a pale stallion that shot fire from its nostrils and the chancel looked like Hades. The Reverend Snider stood up. His face half gone, his chasuble splattered in crimson, he looked at Diamond and beckoned him.

"Diiiiiiaaaamooooonnnn . . ."

Mr. B came in through the wall on a white horse, wearing a crown with a bow in his left hand, aiming straight for John Wayne's head. He fired a single arrow then vaporized.

"Diiiiiiaaaamooooonnnn . . ."

The shot exploded when it hit the cowboy. When the smoke cleared, Michael was on a red horse, swinging a great sword.

Satan was perched behind them with a boom box playing a Biggie Smalls tune, "Suicidal Thoughts."

Cliff came from the back of the church on a black horse, scales in his hands.

"Diiiamon . . . Diiiiiiaaaamon . . . D iiiiie . . ."

"Diamond!"

"Diamond, wake up man," Malik was saying. Siyana was crying.

Diamond got up and sat on the edge of the bed.

"Siyana's getting cranky," Malik said. "It's past her bedtime."

The clock read 1:23 A.M.

"Sharisse is here and we about to go to sleep,"

Malik continued. "You can crash in the living room if you want."

Diamond stared at Malik but couldn't get his bearings through a smog of guilty drowsiness.

"D? You okay?"

"Yeah, yeah," he murmured, put his elbows on his knees, face in his hands, rubbed himself present. "I'm cool."

When he got back to Brooklyn it was well after three A.M.

He was scared to go home. *Maybe I should have taken Tamara's mom up on her offer to spend the night,* he thought. But then his anger got the best of him. *Fuck her, she never cared about me when my ma was alive.*

He walked up the six flights of stairs, dreading every step. They never seemed so long, so quiet, so lonely.

How could he go home to an empty, quiet, dark apartment? He missed the music, the food, his mother. He missed it like a hungry newborn misses its mother's nipple at two in the morning, like an addict with a fifty-dollar-a-day habit misses a fix after six hours, like a convicted felon misses his crew.

When Diamond neared the final corner to the hallway that led to his door, he heard a faint whistling, light as a small chick's chirping early in the morning. The high-pitched frequency was surprisingly on tune, but seemed to come from in between the here and now, the dead and gone. It was the same Marvin Gaye song his mom was humming last week, the last melody he had heard her give the world.

Fuck, he thought, *my mind's playing tricks on me*.

But it wasn't. When he reached his doorstep, he saw his father, hands in his pockets, two battered suitcases on either side of him.

He moved past the whistler without word or acknowledgment. If he was thankful for the company, he didn't know it; couldn't show it.

Cliff picked up his luggage and followed Diamond into the living room, looking around in the dark for an appropriate place to dump his belongings.

"I figure you can sleep here, on the couch," Diamond said and went into his bedroom.

When morning came, father and son sat at the counter at Max and Jack's, an all-night hash joint that served coffee so dark, sludgy, and strong that it could be mistaken for petroleum.

Aside from the essentials, they spoke no words, instead looking out the picture window, making up life histories for passersby in their own minds. It's possible that the men and women making their way down the street had problems of their own, but neither Diamond nor Cliff could see that. They escaped their own uneasiness by accompanying those people to work, school, anywhere, but by the side of a mirror, years removed.

Max was busy scrambling eggs, flipping flapjacks, sizzling links, and shuffling home fries on the griddle. A waitress moved to and fro, refilling coffee, taking orders, cleaning tables, bringing food. There was a line at the take-out counter, with men and women ordering bagels, croissants, and muffins for their jaunts to the workplace.

A disheveled man with a fisherman's hat came in and sat next to Cliff, lit a cigarette, and flipped open the morning edition to the sports page. Cliff immediately began to cough.

"You mind putting that out?" he asked the man.

"You mind coughing somewhere else?" the man retorted.

Annoyed Diamond poked his head over to the man. "Do you mind putting that out?" It was more order than request.

"Geez, a fella can't smoke in peace," the man said, moving down the counter.

A while later, Diamond turned to face his father. "Ma says . . ." he choked on his words, cleared his throat the way you do when you've rehearsed something in your mind, but it still comes out wrong. "She used to say that you could really swing the piano."

Max dropped two platters in front of them—ham and eggs with hash browns and toast.

"I was okay," Cliff said, digging into his breakfast.

"You still play?"

"When I can," he replied. "There's not much work for jazz musicians these days. At least not real jazz musicians. The world has moved on, I'm part of a whole different era."

"You know, I'm a rapper, right?" Diamond

said, finally catching up to his voice. "I got a pretty good shot at landing a record deal."

"Of course you do." Cliff briefly turned to face his son, then shoveled a forkful of eggs into his mouth.

Diamond was put off by his father's casual, almost uninterested manner. *Maybe he's just here for a good breakfast and a few more hours of sack time before he's up and out again.*

"You know," Cliff began after chasing down his breakfast with a hearty gulp of orange juice. "I like what's going on with rap these days. I won't go as far as to vouch for the subject matter at times—it seems to be all hyperbole and ballistics, puns and guns." He turned to his son, getting a bit more comfortable. "Still, I haven't seen such a widespread proliferation, infiltration, and assimilation of the Black experience in mainstream American culture since rock 'n' roll. The way the music, the force has just erupted and affected every aspect of life in this country—it almost makes me want to be young again. You may not be able to appreciate it, 'cause it's always been here for you, but I tell you, the music of your generation has changed the face of life in this country; the whole planet, as a matter of fact."

Diamond had never viewed his art from such a panoramic perspective before. Rapping was what he did, how he expressed himself, maintained his sanity. The fact that he could possibly make a living at it was icing on the cake. To express his thoughts and feelings, prove himself better than the next man, do something that marked him as an individual—that was the carrot dangling from a stick that led him like a mule. He'd never heard anyone, much less someone his father's age, encapsulate, defend, and explain his music with such conviction or eloquence.

"You see, jazz was different," Cliff continued. "It was meant for a select few to understand and comprehend. Yeah, whitey would come around, but he didn't get it—he observed it, eventually packaged and controlled it—but he never *got* it. That's how white folk are—they're enamored by any and everything we do, even when—as a matter of fact, *especially* when—what we do shoots anger and self-determination in the face of his suppression of our liberty as sentient beings."

He glanced at Diamond to make sure his son was still with him. "But you young dudes are raw." He cocked his head back, laughing. "You grip the truth so tightly that even air can't get through your fingers, then you shove your fists right down their throats. And they *eat that shit up.*"

Diamond was mesmerized by his father's words, full of authority, support, and life experience.

"Now," Cliff said, more seriously, "you do have a responsibility to the people to say something of worth, though. To have your voice heard by the world is not only a blessing, it's an obligation. You become a teacher, a leader, maybe even a prophet. It's your own cross to bear. You see, fame and glory are not the reward—they are the vehicles."

Diamond listened intently, mesmerized by his

father's words. He knew that this type of guidance was what he had been missing his whole life. Whatever anger he had felt toward his father was not present at that moment. He felt as whole as a motherless child could feel.

"I'm sorry," Cliff apologized. "I don't mean to come out of nowhere and tell you how to lead your life."

"Nah," Diamond said. "It's cool. I . . . I appreciate it." He turned away for a second, closed his eyes, inhaled quickly, then stared at Max working the grill.

"Coffee?" a waitress asked, coming around with a pot of the crude brew.

Diamond's cup was full, he hadn't even touched his food.

He shook his head to the waitress and dug into his cold meal.

"So why'd you leave?" he asked finally, wiping his lips with his napkin.

Cliff turned on his stool and looked Diamond dead in his eyes.

"I have a lot excuses for what I did," he said solemnly. "But no reasons. The best I can do is tell you my story, let you know what was on my mind, and hope . . . I don't know what I hope. But if you want to listen, I'll tell it."

Diamond didn't answer, but Cliff knew himself well enough to know that his son's silence granted permission to tell the tale.

"Before I met your mother, I spent my whole life on the road trying to make it as a jazz pianist," Cliff said. "But my whole life changed when I met your mom. She was damn near the most beautiful thing I had ever seen in my life, unlike any woman I had ever met. There was something special about her. The way she smiled, the way her face lit up a room."

Perhaps it was Diamond's imagination, but his father's facial muscles seemed to visibly loosen like soil in a warm summer rain.

"Now, I'm sure that I don't have to tell you how many women you can get as a musician," Cliff continued. "It was a different woman every night—and they didn't mind the brevity of our relationships one bit.

"But your mother—your mother was different. She was no one-night stand. I was in love with her from the second I saw her. I mean *love*, Diamond. Love." He was somewhere else as he spoke those words.

"I promised her that we'd settle down together when I could break out of the chitlin circuit. There wasn't anything I couldn't do with your mother by my side or at my back. I was invincible."

He continued his story, but dark clouds formed over his words as he spoke of how work became scarce, and how, though he couldn't realize it back then, he secretly blamed Rose for ruining his career. He unwittingly took his anger out on her, his frustration with himself chased her further and further away, until she was set to leave him.

"I couldn't have that," Cliff confessed. "My woman was all I had. I refused to lose her, too."

He married Rose quickly, believing that would make things better. And it did for a while. Being a husband gave Cliff a renewed sense of self. He signed a deal as a producer with a small record label in Chicago and traveled across time zones, making some of the best music of his life. After about a year, Rose became pregnant.

"There's something about having another life in the world that increases your power and gives you insight that you didn't have before," Cliff offered.

He soon found out that he was not getting his proper share of monies for his records; that he didn't own any of his publishing or rights to the music he created.

Cliff's face stiffened and grew malevolent.

"I went right in there and told that overblown cracker that he had better give me what I had coming to me or I would quit working. But I had signed a contract. I had been so happy when I was first signing that I didn't look at the fine print. It was like cattle slavery—they *owned* me as a producer." Cliff grunted at the thought. "No other label would touch me, lest they'd get sued. And I refused to record for that fat boy anymore. I was stuck.

"I came back to New York," he continued. As rush hour was over, the diner had emptied of patrons. "By this time I started hitting the bottle pretty hard. Your mom was five months' pregnant with you. I tried working straight jobs to get enough money for us all to live on. It worked for a minute, but it made me miserable—I'm not cut of the cloth that makes one employable."

Cliff hung his head. The memory was weighing

him down like an anchor of guilt. "I began taking it all out on your mom, again. That's one thing about Black men—the only thing this damned country gives us power over is our women. I think Black women realize this, which is why they take so much shit from us.

"Your mom, God bless her, was the best cheerleader, helping me to get my life back in order. But it's a vicious cycle: The more she tried to help me, the worse I got. I began to feel like I wasn't worthy of her or her love. And when nothing would happen, I drank till I was numb."

Cliff had grown tired of taking handouts from people, of having Rose being the sole provider for the family. One day after a failed job interview, he walked into a bar and drank till closing. When he couldn't pay his tab, a few toughs took him outside behind an alley and beat him senseless. When he came to, it was the next morning. He went to a friend and borrowed some money. Then, he was on the first thing smoking out of town.

"I don't know who I was running from, her or me," he confessed heavily. "I must have been gone a year before it finally hit me that I could not come back. Not after leaving like that, I couldn't."

"How could you live like that?" Diamond asked.

"I don't know. It wasn't easy." Cliff shook his head. "I'm not exactly what you pictured, am I?"

"Ma never told me you had a drinking problem. But she did talk about how fly you was on the ivory. Said you were the baddest piano player she ever heard. She used to say I got my looks from her and my talent from you," Diamond smiled.

"I've never heard you play, but I sure as hell know you ain't got her looks," said Cliff, releasing an easy chuckle.

Diamond grinned back at him.

"So how are you with the sauce now?" Diamond asked with genuine concern.

"I haven't touched a drink in fourteen years," his father said proudly, knocking on the counter.

Later that night, Diamond was back in SuperTracks, the lyrics coming from him like snowflakes in a blizzard.

I got the handskills to fill landfills / From when I packed the deuce-fifth in my Grant Hills / Tell your man chill / 'Fore he's a corpse / It's the full force / Like downing a case of Crazy Horse . . .

"No, no, no!" Diamond yelled into the mic, flinging his headphones in disgust. "This is all wrong." He walked behind the soundboard where Baz sat, tried and tired.

"We've been here for six hours," the engineer complained. "And you still haven't liked a thing."

"Well if it ain't right, it ain't right."

"Whatever," Baz said, closing his bloodshot eyes and resting his head on the console.

"Fuck it," Diamond said, exasperated. "We ain't getting nothing done here tonight. I want you in here early tommorow."

He began packing his notebooks.

Baz sucked his teeth. "Just remember that I ain't been paid in weeks."

"You think I don't know you ain't been paid, nigga?" Diamond spat.

"I'm just saying . . ." Baz mumbled. "You got me working all day an' shit—"

"Listen!" Diamond shouted. "This is not a fuckin' game with me, okay."

Baz was startled and scared by the sudden outburst. He just stared at Diamond with his mouth open.

"Just so we have an understanding," Diamond said in a quivering low tone. "You will be here by no later than eleven A.M. tomorrow. If not," Diamond slowly clenched his fists in front of him, closed his eyes, and let out a deep sigh. Then he pleaded with Baz. "Please, just be here early tomorrow. I don't know what I'll do to you if you're not here." His eyes glassed over.

What the fuck? Baz thought. *I'm not even gettin' paid and now this nigga's threatening me!*

"Whatever," he said, turning up his lips.

WATCHU WANNA DO?
(12" GAGE REMIX)

Diamond was not ready to go home. Not yet. He wanted to talk to his father badly, but needed to distance himself from the situation. Part of him wanted to, actually *needed* to, be angry at Cliff. Or at least he wanted his dad to think he was angry.

He met up with Gage at the Barracuda Lounge. The place was hopping, packed from wall to wall with leagues of producers, artists, and groupies.

Gage was by a small table overlooking the dance floor. He had a bird's-eye view of all the attention being given to the studio gangsters, posers, and wanna-bes. Men in slick suits buzzed around the flavors-of-the-month like flies on feces, while eager women advertised their availability. Gage found no amusement in the unabashed flattery and ass kissing.

"Man these motherfuckers ain't got shit on you lyrically," he said to Diamond, pointing to the huddled cliques. "Just watch, I'ma make you larger than any of these bitches."

Diamond surveyed the scene—he had no idea

what Michael was talking about. He'd been questioning his friend's judgment more and more as of late. As a criminal, Michael was leading them down a dark road, from which there was no turning back. As a manager, he made a smart criminal.

"You know my old man used to play some pretty dope jazz, right?" Diamond asked, changing the subject.

"You finally coming around, huh?" Gage chuckled. "I'm telling you—only a man can raise a man to be a man."

Michael's logic was rudimentary but couldn't be denied. A few short hours with his father and Diamond was already beginning to think for himself. The two turned their attention to a pair of shadows seductively entwining themselves around each other on the dance floor.

Gage sucked back the rest of his beer, draining the bottle.

The two women laughed between themselves before sauntering over to the table where the boys sat. Jeannine was wearing a low-cut brown dress, its neckline plunging down between her ample breasts. Keisha was wearing a fire red sequined number, which matched the shine of her perpetually moist lips.

"What's up, baby?" Jeannine purred seductively, leaning down to give Gage an eyeful of her considerable assets. "How come you didn't call me on Sunday?"

Gage grinned slyly at Diamond. "Me and D decided we would go to the House of the Lord and worship—you know it's kinda like a tradition for us."

Diamond was incensed. Though no one suspected them, their caper had been front-page news. If Gage kept dropping hints, a woman as smart as Jeannine would put one and one together. She'd be sure to tell Keisha, who'd crack under the whisper of a threat from the authorities.

"Uh-huh," Keisha moaned with a coarse throat. What she lacked in intelligence she more than made up for in sex appeal. She slinked to Diamond like a walking python, slowly running his cheek with sculptured nails.

"Beep me tonight, Gage," Jeannine said, each word dripping with intent. "I don't want to be alone."

"Neither do I," added Keisha with a wink.

"Maybe the two of you could hook up and play cards," Diamond spat, a bit annoyed by the seductive display.

"Don't mind him," Gage said through heavy eyelids. "I got you tonight—both of you, if necessary."

The girls smiled and walked away, asses swaying side to side.

"What's your problem tonight?" Gage asked, once the girls were out of view.

"Nothing," Diamond brushed off his friend's inquiry. "I'm going to get a soda. You want one?"

"Nah—get me another beer."

When Diamond had left, Gage's attention was riveted on a table halfway across the club, where

Mr. White, Platinum's record executive, sat for drinks with Mr. B.

The power brokers were engrossed in deep conversation when they were interrupted.

"What's up, Mr. B?" Gage asked, hovering over the table.

Mr. B gave a polite smile. "Gage, whatever are you doing in a fine establishment like this?"

"You know, like you all, I was just kicking it, getting my groove on."

Mr. B sighed like a single mother interrupted by her toddler just as she was about to consummate a relationship. The old gangster prepared to introduce the boy to Mr. White but was cut off.

"We've already met," said Gage, respectfully.

"Have we?" Mr. White peered at Gage, trying to place his face.

"Yeah, last week. I introduced you to my man Diamond. You remember, you wanted to hear his demo tape."

"He's a rapper, right?" asked Mr. White, rubbing his cheek reflectively.

"He's for real, Mr. White," Gage replied, enthusiastically.

Mr. B concurred. "You should really hear this kid, Will. Fix him up with a manager, help him get some direction or something—that's all he really needs."

"I'm his manager," Gage piped up.

Mr. B burst out laughing, giving the ever-present sour look on his face an even more putrid appearance—it looked like his face was about to crack.

After he had calmed down, Mr. B asked matter-of-factly: "What do you know about the music business?"

"Look at all the motherfuckers in this place." Gage spread his arms like a departing eagle. "All they doing is frontin' 'bout the same shit—money, drugs, guns, and hoes. I know all about that real shit."

White shook his head despondently. "You're not going to go far in this industry with that kind of attitude, I can tell you right now."

"Look where it got you," Gage responded defiantly.

"Gage, go back and sit down," Mr. B ordered. "You weren't invited here and you've more than overstayed your unwelcome."

When Gage returned to his table, Diamond was nervously sipping on a soda.

"Told you, you going soft," Gage said as he sat down heavily, noting his friend's choice of beverage, then taking a long pull from his beer.

Diamond ignored the glib comment. "What the fuck just happened?"

"Let me tell you something, son," Gage began with determination. "I'm tired of playing everybody's dumb-ass games. Look, you want to be a superstar, am I right?"

Diamond said nothing.

"Then fuck that demo shit, son."

"What are you talking about?" Diamond asked. He knew that without a demo tape, the hopes of getting signed with a major label were very slim.

"How many tracks you made so far?"

"There's only three that I'm feeling. But you need at least five if you want your demo taken seriously. But after talking to my pops, I'm not even sure if I'm feeling the three that I got."

"Never mind that." Gage's eyes flashed as he leaned in closer. "You need five tracks for a demo tape, right?"

"Uh-huh." Diamond was curious where this was going.

"But you only need six for an EP."

Diamond was fixed on the words, but he still didn't get it.

"You hear what I'm saying?" Gage asked.

"Nah."

Gage laughed. "Son, we can press the CD on our own independent label! That's where the money's at, anyway."

Diamond shook his head. "Man, I can't even get enough money to finish my demo, how we gonna start a record label?"

"Well, we did pretty good at that church—and there's a lot more Sundays in the year." Gage raised his eyebrows knowingly.

"I ain't down with that," Diamond said, startling Gage with his intensity.

"Look, the only other way you gonna get a record deal is if you suck Mr. White's dick," Gage scoffed.

Diamond leapt to his feet, knocking the table over. Gage's hand shot to the handle of the .45 he had stuck in his waistband.

The patrons near the table, no strangers to gun-play, backed away quickly.

Diamond stood there panting heavily, his eyes locked on Gage's. Gage kept his hand on his piece, not backing down an inch either. He looked as if he was begging Diamond to make a move, forget-ting that he was his best friend. Instead, Gage let himself get caught up in the challenge of being fronted, and he did not want to appear soft.

Diamond saw it in Gage's eyes, just then, his best friend, his childhood buddy, seemed like a stranger to him.

"Fuck this shit!" he yelled pushing past Gage and storming out of the club.

Gage hitched his pants, righted his seat, and sat back down, smugly for the benefit of the on-lookers, who began to mill around once again, sidestepping the overturned table. Although he appeared self-satisfied, Gage knew he made a mis-take with Diamond. He had let his temper, and his ego, get to him. He sat there in the din of the club, and motioned for the waitress to bring him another drink.

MURDER THEM

Jeannine had not known Gage, as the thugs and those in the drug world chose to address Michael Williams. She had known *of* him. Known *of* him that word-of-mouth way you know of the summer blockbuster before you've seen it; the way you know how your neighbor's new car drives after he's spoken of it ad infinitum; the way aspiring street hoods know of Scarface—known of, perhaps seen, definitely researched, but never met, intimated with, had coffee, tea, or blunts with. No, no. Nothing firsthand, nothing where one could tell the up close and personal details like a chipped tooth, a smile that could scare Satan, a left eye that twitches in electrical storms.

What Jeannine knew of Gage was more like what you would gain from a character in a poorly written novel—one-dimensional tales of who he was, stories of the enigmatic, obscurely drawn figures that he broke bread with, how he shot his mother in the face with a nine millimeter in broad daylight after she asked for some free crack, that he was raised by the wolves to become, perhaps the deadliest predator on Brooklyn's piss-stained sidewalk Serengeti. The flame of the lore attracted her like a Black Butterfly.

Of course, deep in her subconscious, she had asked for such a manchild to appear in her world; she wanted a thug nigga. Word on the streets is that every woman does. (Not coincidentally, the streets where the word comes from is heavily populated by cats that laugh at the Dark Lord himself through the haze of blunt smoke escaping from their bejeweled ivories and pack mini-cannons in their caskets just in case he remembers their faces when they meet again.) They say that the ladies are magnetized by that crude mix of bottom-shelf ingredients: roughness, mercilessness, the drive to do what others won't; the ability to be given the vilest "why," which must be done, and to fill the void no matter who, when, what, where, or how, without a fluctuation in breath. They say this is what the ladies want.

It was Gage who had interrupted that bank manager (what was his name?) at the bar, just as he was about to make his suggestion, his swift swoop for the kill like a hungry raptor. He had been supplying her with drinks all night and she stayed glued to her stool just as surely as there where twenty-carat diamonds embedded in the bezel of his Breitling. Yet, like the salesman he must be during the day, the wind-up came right before his pitch, obvious as Gooden on the mound. She felt it in the temperature of his eyes looking down her terrific bust, saw it in his body language when he admired the craftsmanship of the spaghetti-thin straps on her summer dress and complimented her small neat waist, saw it again when he shifted in his stool to get a look at those legs that went on forever. So, the banker—we'll call him Raoul, because Jeannine would never want to forget a name. Raoul was ready to close the deal, to make his own deposit with the hopes of seeing her interest rate rise (without causing inflation, of course), to go for that Employee of the Month Award, when in came Gage—pure attitude underneath a black bowler hat, crisp white shirt and white Gucci pants (Jeannine could tell they were Gucci by the cut), black suede loafers with the gold Gucci insignia.

He got class, she thought. He filled the outfit with a comfort and confidence that was all sexual—low-groan-in-the-back-of-your-throat sexual, cross-your-legs-and-rinse-your-panties-in-the-sink sexual.

He had all the defiance of a Taurus, just so *right* about everything when he spoke. *Did he even see Raoul? Did he hear the conversation? They must be in it together*, she had decided at last, 'cause there was no way Gage could know what she was thinking, what she had been thinking about for the past thirty minutes, the fears she believed locked underneath layers of Amaretto and orange juice, the things she had wanted to hear, the questions that made her laugh from the belly, and the touch—slight and slow, from mid-bicep to inner elbow, that made her recross her legs for the third time since she had seen him. No. There was no way Gage should have seen that.

And, by all rights, he didn't. Michael Williams had saved his Gage face for Raoul, the spineless, heartless thing right behind him, who had neither the nerve to tap the young man and question his intrusion on the conversation that he was having with the young lady before he was so rudely interrupted, nor the brightness to get up and go home.

Jeannine had not known Michael, never even heard of him. Too bad, Michael was the real thug. Michael was the one who calculated, plotted, and thought. Michael was the one who kept his mouth shut. He was one hundred times more deadly, thuggish, and ruggish than a million Gages on their best day—almost as dangerous as Diamond. Gage was all pomp and circumstance, show and tell, an act.

Michael was the hamster in the wheel that powered the whole machinery of madness. The hate that Hate cut from its womb and let loose on the world, cultured enough to analyze, define, and direct, educated enough to add one and one and still have one, wise enough to decipher conversations by slipping into a privileged colloquialism, yet strong enough to—through all the trials and tribulations, heavens and hells, sunshines and rains—remain, indubitably, undeniably, sane.

It was Michael who sat in the Barracuda that night stewing in his own inebriated thoughts, a few hours after Diamond had stalked off, just after his best friend had confronted him for the second time in just as many days. Michael's form of Darwinism left him feeling no different about the clergyman whose occipital lobe was removed by one half of the twin arms that got thrown into a green dumpster in Coney Island. For Michael had had no choice—he and Diamond went to do a job and were compromised. What else could he do—turn himself in? It was Reverend Snider's death before his dishonor—plain and simple. But Gage—Gage used an unsavory moment for self-gratification. Perhaps it was his lot in life. But there was not much time for such Aristotelian theorization, because when he saw the milk and caramel contrast of Jeannine's skin and dress, his sweet tooth took over.

Jeannine was a curvaceous silhouette talking to Hollis to one side of the dance floor. Gage's anger rose like water in a flood, with each adoring tilt of her head, each impressed giggle she let off. The extravagant dealer slid his gilded hand over dime piece's delicate fingers and whispered in her ear. She giggled again, more playfully this time than before. If he had not been drinking, Gage would have stormed in like the Allied troops on D-Day to regain his territory. But he had sipped himself past the point of stupidity after his fourth beer. The Russian quaaludes that he'd been downing since made him calm and detached, almost as if he were watching the events thrown onto a life-size screen through a movie projector.

Gage sat there watching Hollis make time, a devious plan forming behind his glazed eyes. Jealousy had no business here.

Hollis made a suggestive tug at Jeannine's

waist, which almost pulled her onto him. An outside observer could have bet the farm that Gage had lost any connection to reality. He sat there in the dark of the club, drunk off his own thoughts more than any liquor, smiling lowly at the occurrences. Jeannine pushed back and waved her finger back and forth at Hollis. When he was far enough away, she began to smile to no one in particular and danced with herself. Her body was the tongue of a yawning lion, lapping up the attention of every man on the tiled floor. Hungrily, Hollis moved in for the kill. When Jeannine turned to the wall and ignored him, he pulled behind her so close that his hump poked her crack, and then he planted a wet tongue in her ear before heading toward the bathroom.

When Gage was upon her, he squeezed her elbow with force.

"Ow! Damn, Gage!" she squealed at first, then got her bearings. "Did I do something to upset you, baby?"

"No, you're doing quite fine, actually." His eyes darted around frantically, but his demeanor was cool as sipping iced drinks with umbrellas in them on a yacht. "Are you having fun?"

"I could be having more fun with you."

"That will have to wait. What was Hollis saying to you?"

"Nothing."

"Nothing about what?"

"Nothing about nothing."

"You never were a good liar. That's why your

176

mom says the things she says to you. She's not a good liar either."

Jeannine was struck frozen. She had not told Gage much about her relationship with her mother, especially about the lack of trust between them. *How does he know?* She stared deeply to hold back the tears.

"So, what were you and Hollis talking about?"

"You asked before and I told you: Nothing."

Veins protruded from Gage's temples as he tightened his grip on Jeannine's arm.

"Okay, okay, he wanted me to come to his place to a party." She winced and whined. "Now let me go."

"Yeah a party of two and guess who's coming," Gage said, as his fingers stayed locked on Jeannine's fragile elbow.

"I told him no, baby. I told him I wasn't gonna go."

Gage gave no answer.

"I told him I wasn't into it, okay? Now let's you and I . . ."

Gage silenced her with a raised finger from his free hand. "You go back over there and tell that horny little motherfucker that you changed your mind, that you will be at his place a little later. Make sure you get his address and number, not the cell phone either, okay. But don't give that motherfucker your own number, you understand me? If he asks for it, tell him that your boyfriend picks up your phone and give him your beeper number."

"I know what to do."

When he was assured of her ability, he released her elbow.

"I'll be waiting for you outside. Don't fuck up girl, or it will be your ass."

Cliff was haunted by what could have been as he lay on the sofa in his son's apartment. Though he wore nothing but a tank top and shorts, he sweated profusely. He got up, made his way to what used to be Rose's bedroom, and slowly stepped inside. The bedspread was smooth; the closet still filled with simple yet effective ten-dollar dresses. On the nightstand was a framed photo of Rose when she was around Diamond's age. The pic was taken at Coney Island, where Rose and Cliff had gone one summer. The Cyclone, Nathan's, the boardwalk—it was a glorious day, with the sun warming the sand under their toes as they sat on the beach. Rose's long wind-swept hair blew around her young face, caressing it like a cloud. *God*, he thought, *she was beautiful.* He shut his eyes and breathed in deeply. She smelled just as he remembered.

Hollis was half-dressed with a towel around his waist when he scrambled over to the intercom to let Jeannine in.

"Damn, you're early, girl, but I like an eager woman." He watched as she walked past the lobby security camera, her black-and-white image slithering by on his intercom unit. Hollis was too busy licking his lips and rubbing his hands to notice the way she stuck a MetroCard in between the door and the bolt to keep the front gate from locking.

When Jeannine entered the apartment, she walked like she had too much too drink, wobbling lightly on her heels and laughing at anything. There was a glass stained with three different shades of lipstick. She figured whoever had been there before had spent a long time drinking with Hollis. It infuriated her that she had been Hollis's second choice. It caused her even more burn that the jovial, bathrobed player next to her either didn't care if he got caught or was just not up on his game.

She tuned in to the Barry White song playing on the stereo, and adjusted to the soft lighting. What kept her going, what kept her staying, what kept her, was the feeling she had coming up the steps. She felt purpose, albeit deadly. She was no longer an observer to Gage's world, she was in it. That alone was aphrodisiac enough to endure whatever it was that Gage wanted her to do.

"I didn't think you'd make it."

"I did say I'd come, didn't I?"

"Yeah."

"Why, do girls often turn you down?"

Hollis dove into the valley between her peaks with a wet tongue. "Women never turn me down," he slurped.

Jeannine had been pawed at, caressed, and penetrated by an unmanicured finger by the time there was a soft knock at the door.

"Don't you think you should get that?" Jeannine asked. "It's not your wife is it?"

"Could be . . . but she could spend the night outside." He smiled and stuck his head under her short dress, between her legs, his tongue making its way to heaven.

The tapping at the door returned.

Jeannine got up and slinked over to the door. "I'll get it," she said. Then with a smile, "Sometime's three's company."

The thought of the ménage à trois would be the last happy thought Hollis would have. When Jeannine turned the door handle, Gage exploded through, bending it off one of its hinges. Hollis reeled backward, tripping onto his buttocks.

"Are you Tony?" the masked assailant yelled.

Naturally, Hollis was more than happy to respond in the negative. He was not Tony, thankfully. The chrome .45 in his eye bought him back to sobriety. His breathing was understandably uncontrollable. A Molotov of fear and adrenaline rushed out of his drawers, trickling down his thigh, letting him know: You are wide awake. For the moment.

"Get up bitch!" Gage commanded.

"I said I'm not Tony!" Hollis cried and Gage pistol-whipped him. Hollis struggled to his feet, gasping. "Please don't hurt me."

"I want everything you got," Gage said, taking inventory of the luxurious apartment.

Hollis was led through the apartment; lavish room by lavish room, collecting money and his possessions for the masked intruder, who insulted him at every turn and some straightaways.

"This everything I got man," Hollis pleaded,

after accumulating a heap of jewels, watches, and cash. "I swear, this is all I got on me!"

Gage surveyed the stash. He didn't believe Hollis, but his take was more than enough for his purposes. He turned to Jeannine, whose eyes pulsed with excitement. She looked so frightened and inviting that Gage wanted to tie Hollis to a chair and make him watch while they did the do, just to show him what he missed. But then, he saw the line of dried liquid stuck to Jeannine's inner thigh.

It made him insanely jealous.

"By the way," he said, turning to face the quivering man, removing his mask. "Thanks a lot, Hollis." With that, Gage raised the gun and placed it directly between Hollis's widening eyes. Hollis's face was paralyzed by terror, and he pleaded soundlessly out of his mouth. Gage regarded him for a second, relishing the power he was exerting over this sad brother, and pulled the trigger, sending him sprawling backward in a shower of blood, bone, and brains.

GHETTO SUPASTAR
(AFTER HOURS MIX)

Cliff was still sweating, still could not sleep, and paced the living room of Diamond's apartment, looking insidiously over at his two suitcases that lay in the far corner of the room. The sun would be coming up soon, and the room was filled with the fuzzy light of a brightening sky. Finally, he walked over to one of the suitcases, and opening it up, extracted a large plastic bag from the inside. Opening its Zip-loc seal, he sat down on the couch again, taking a syringe out of the bag.

Diamond had been cruising around for a while, trying to shrug off what had happened between him and Gage at the club. There was no excuse. Gage tried to play him, and let his anger get in the way of his reason. Again. Diamond wasn't sure how much more he could take of Gage's hot head and grand designs, the ones that usually involved getting them both nearly killed.

Killing the engine of the Cutlass, Diamond made his way into his building and up the stairs. It was early in the morning, so he took care to

tread the hallway softly so he wouldn't wake anyone up on the floor, especially Cliff.

Diamond slid his key quietly into the lock of
his apartment, closing the door gently behind him.
Stepping into the living room, he saw Cliff, his
head focused on a needle going in his arm.

Diamond was incensed. "Fuck, man!" he yelled,
not caring who he woke up now. "How can you
be doing this shit! You said you were straight, and
I believed you!"

Cliff barely looked over as he continued to
squeeze the head of the syringe until the milky
liquid inside had completely emptied into his
vein.

"I don't need no father strung out on dope in
my apartment. Take your shit and get the fuck
out of here."

Cliff pushed the needle carefully out of his arm,
placing a dry cloth over the vein to sop up the
welling blood. Without looking up at Diamond,
he said quietly, "I'm a diabetic."

Diamond did a double take and moved in closer
to take a look. It was then he noticed the small
vial of insulin on the coffee table.

"Geez, Cliff, what was I supposed to think?"

"Do I look like a junkie to you? Or is that just
what you expect of me?"

"It ain't like that. I just don't know what to
think anymore."

Diamond walked past his father and proceeded
down the hall to his room. It had been a long
night. Diamond lay in bed and stared up at the

ceiling of his bedroom, knowing that, like his father in the next room, sleep would prove hard.

It was the harsh ring of the telephone that woke him a few hours later. With his eyes half closed, Diamond reached over gingerly and picked up the receiver.

"Yeah . . . no . . ." he intoned, his voice gravely and rough. "No, I'm awake. Okay, I'll come over. Yeah, said I'm coming over. Right now."

Groggy and discombobulated, Diamond got up and stumbled into the living room, expecting to see Cliff crashed out on the sofa. But the bed linen Diamond gave him was folded neatly on one of the cushions, the pillow placed on top of them. His suitcases were put off to one side, out of the way. Rubbing his stomach and yawning, Diamond wondered where Cliff might be.

Around the corner, Cliff had just walked into a seedy little piano bar. Although the dark, sullied bar was filled with smoke, there was only one patron, a pasty-faced old man in flannel, hunched over the bar with a cigarette dangling from his lips, a full ashtray and a half-drunk beer in front of him.

Cliff walked in and ran his large hand down the bar's scarred surface. The bartender, who was busy drying glasses, turned around to face Cliff as he approached.

"What can I get you?"

"Whiskey, straight," Cliff answered, nodding hello to the old regular.

The bartender took a bottle of Jim Beam off the shelf and poured a generous shot.

Cliff motioned toward the old dusty piano sitting in the corner of the bar. "Is she still in tune?"

The bartender looked over at the piano as if noticing it for the first time. "To tell you the truth, I don't know. It's been a while since anyone has played anything in here."

"Mind if I give it a try?"

"Knock yourself out."

Cliff just stared at his shot of Beam with a sad, nostalgic look before walking over to the piano. Placing the whiskey on its worn surface, Cliff lifted the keyboard guard and began to explore the eroded keys. A few of the high sharps were missing and she seemed to be a little out of tune. It was an ancient Steinway, with cigarette burns, splintered legs, and a shaky stool. Cliff pressed down on a couple of keys, playing half of a short major scale. The action was weak, but he knew he could bang out a few tunes, if he was so inclined.

Cliff looked at the warm and inviting brown liquid resting on the piano, like a beacon leading him to the past. He could remember the heavenly burning of bourbon sliding down his throat, the calming warm that spread through his chest afterward, the familiar sense of false ease the liquor gave him. The allure was almost too strong. It had been a while since Cliff had a drink; one sip could lead him back off the wagon. He had woken up with a thirst, confused and depressed about his situation in life, and now, as he sat eyeing the glass, he wondered if it would be worth it after all.

No time for thought—he quickly banged out a few jazz chords. The mellow sound reverberated through the bar, almost changing its atmosphere— what was a dirty dive of a bar, usually filled with dust and rotting livers, felt like a downscale jazz club during off-hours. Cliff worked his way up and down the eighty-eight pieces of ivory. A tune surfaced in his memory, an old jazz standard by Duke Ellington. His hands gained momentum as they flowed like waves over the decrepit keys, the music swelling with rapturous intensity. Even the bartender and the lonely patron turned to watch in stunned silence, uplifted by the beautiful sounds coming from the hunk of dead wood.

Cliff was totally lost in his own world as he played soulful, funky, syncopated jazz tunes. One after another, they flowed from him as if from a blocked spring, now bubbling forth with sweet musical ambrosia. His soul infused his fingers, and his solo reached a transcendent crescendo. The bartender looked on incredulously. The old man had closed his eyes and seemed lost in his thoughts. The song ended and the music seemed to hang in the air with the smoke as it faded. Cliff's hands fell heavily down to his lap, as if they were burning with embarrassment. He looked forward, taking a deep breath, then rose and walked out of the bar.

The glass full of whiskey on the piano was still reverberating from the echoes of Cliff's music.

WATCHU WANNA DO?
(REAL LIVE)

Diamond was waiting outside Tamara's apartment with a wide grin on his face when she opened the door. She had planned on doing some shopping before Diamond came over, but couldn't find her grocery list. So she was frustrated from the jump.

Diamond swept her into his arms, kissing her deeply. Tamara resisted as best as she could, but soon surrendered as his sweet and tender advances melted her resolve.

"I know what you need, baby," Diamond whispered as they finally parted.

He lifted her in his arms and carried her upstairs. Tamara smiled coyly at her man, and before she knew it, Diamond had deftly slipped off her T-shirt and was planting soft, firm kisses on her perky breasts.

"Honey, I like what you're doing to me but this is not why I called you over."

"That's alright," Diamond smiled. "We just have a change in plans."

"Diamond," Tamara brought him to attention with the tone of her voice. She backed away from her boyfriend.

"I'm pregnant."

"Are you sure?"

Tamara nodded her head meekly. Diamond stood up and began to pace, thinking hard.

"No. I mean, are you really sure?" Diamond asked again.

"You want me to show you the little stick I peed on?"

"You know, those things aren't always accurate."

"I peed on six of them. I'm pregnant."

"How . . . how did it . . ."

"If you're asking me how it happened . . ."

"I thought you were on the pill?"

"I was."

"What happened?"

"You try taking those little colored pills every day when you only see your man twice a month. See how long you stick with it." Then, "Why am I being blamed for this?"

"Look, what am I supposed to do, here? Just tell me—what am I supposed to be saying in a situation like this?"

"I don't know—maybe you could just hold me, tell me you love me. Tell me that whatever I choose, you'll be there for me." Her words were a lot stronger than she was—tears began to well up in her gorgeous dark eyes.

"Choose? I ain't ready to be no father, baby."

"Not ready, or not willing? It's a world of difference."

Diamond took a deep breath and calmed his words. "I just have too many things I wanna do with my life. I'll drive you to the appointment, okay?"

Tamara got up from the sofa incensed. "You're a real shit, you know that?"

"I'm just being real."

There was a forever silence in the room. Then, Tamara asked, "Do you love me Diamond?"

"You know how I feel about you."

"No, listen to me, Diamond, 'cause I asked a specific question—*do you love me?*" Diamond just looked down at his shoes, trying to avoid Tamara's burning eyes. "Why are you having a hard time saying it? When we were bumpin' and grindin' and getting all nasty and freaky you were saying it to me nonstop!"

"Look, if you want me to say it, I'll say it, okay?"

"You'd just be mimicking my words like a trained chimpanzee, which is exactly what I think of you right now." Tamara gave him a look that could cut through steel. "I don't need this, so why don't you just leave."

"Baby that's cold."

"And it's gonna get a whole lot colder if you don't get your sorry ass out of my place."

"But baby I . . ."

"Just go!" she yelled, tears streaming down her face.

Diamond backed up toward the door, his mind reeling. It was as if he'd stepped across an invisible line with Tamara, and he knew she wouldn't let him back into her good graces.

"Alright, I'm outta here," he finally said, not knowing what else to do. "I'll check you later."

"Don't bother," said Tamara bluntly, and slammed the door behind him.

Back in her apartment, Tamara collapsed against the door and burst into tears. Outside the door, Diamond, who hadn't moved, listened to Tamara's wails and felt the door shake as her body was wracked with sobs. After a few minutes, he headed down the front steps.

Driving down the street in the Cutlass, Diamond was completely absorbed in the thoughts swirling around in his head. First his mother, then his father, and now this. Diamond just couldn't believe Tamara was pregnant. She was obviously not screwing around on him, so he was very definitely screwed. How many people did he know himself that were pregnant before they were twenty? How many women did he know that got knocked up by some brother down the street, only to never hear from the man again? Now he was one of them.

He thought about Tamara. Sure, he loved being with her. She was beautiful, smart, and a stone-cold polecat in the bedroom. But did he love her enough so that she would be the only one? Especially now, before his music career caught on fire and took off like a bottle rocket? But did he even have a choice now? How many people in the hood have had to face this very decision? When faced with a similar situation, people became primal— it's purely fight or flight. Diamond thought that he should just take off. Avoid the whole situation; move to LA, maybe out on the coast, where there's a record producer on every corner.

But wouldn't he just be doing what his own father did to him? And to his mother? What about his mother—the woman who scrimped and saved and worked her fingers sore, just to provide him with a decent home and food on the table? After his own father ran out on them, his mother became a rock for Diamond, teaching him right from wrong, guiding him righteously and firmly, but lovingly. Now, like his own mother, wouldn't Tamara have to face this alone? Like a lone ship tossed on stormy seas? Would he abandon his own mother in a situation like this?

Diamond drove for hours, absorbing the life out on the streets, turning his attention outward instead of to the turbulent whirlpool inside his head. The hood came alive around him. Its energy seemingly propelling the Cutlass down the street. Old people lumbered in the crosswalks, their faces empty, their eyes vacant. In the alleyways, rusted cars sat on cinder blocks, stripped and ripped up, often with someone sleeping inside them. Dilapidated buildings with rotting signs, trash heaped in convenient corners in dead ends. Hard stares.

Diamond drove on. Trees, though few and far between, seemed lush in the warm breeze. A group of shorties strolled by, some skipping with their backpacks, laughing and teasing each other on the way home from school. A mother sat on a stoop, baby cradled in her arms, tilting a bottle to its mouth. An older woman in an old green knit shawl leaned out a window above, talking to the mother while fanning herself. Another baby's cries could be heard from another window.

Diamond circled the streets endlessly, watching, thinking. He passed a local ball court, all chain-link and asphalt, and checked out a pick-up game being played out by teenagers, with the intensity of a Knicks-Bulls playoff game. He saw the people on the bench, cheering and macking, jeering and laughing. Diamond watched the eyes of the people he passed on the street. They were filled with joy, concern, pain, deceit, and despair.

And hope.

FOR THE LOVE OF THIS
(NO FORWARDS)

The music thumped and Baz was getting jiggy with it. Wearing mixing headphones and wiping his nose, he sat at the console flipping switches and turning knobs. Wincing to a pitch he turned up way too high, Baz danced over to one side of the board and readjusted everything, nervously looking over at the dancing levels on the equalizer. He was screwing things up, bad.

Diamond sat in the background on a stool, listening through another pair of headphones that were plugged directly into the board. Baz continued to fumble while trying to set the levels on the various tracks. The bass suddenly became louder and louder, overpowering the percussion and drowning out the sound of Diamond's rhymes.

Diamond tore his headphones off in frustration. "No, no, man! What the fuck is this shit? All I hear is freaking bass!"

"Chill," replied Baz, trying to diffuse the situation. "This shit is hot, D. That's the new sound, baby. It's the real thing right there."

"Yo, yo, yo Baz. You can't even hear the words. I didn't know blow messed your ears as well as your nose," Diamond seethed.

"Nah, man, I'm tellin' you, this is the sound," Baz tried, his eyes downcast. Diamond looked away, shaking his head, when he saw Marshall standing with his arms crossed at the studio door.

"D, we gotta talk," he said, and turned to walk away.

Diamond spun on Baz. "Look, fix the bass, alright?" he said, then he followed Marshall out the door.

As he walked down the hall toward Marshall's office, Diamond looked at all the framed gold records lining he walls, gifts from recording artists who hit it big. Such was Marshall's respect, that even the most popular rap artist, basking in money and fame and drugs and women, would remember who let them cut their first tracks, often for free. They would recall their humble beginnings in Brooklyn, and the man who nurtured their dreams. One day, when he got his big deal, Diamond would be sure to send Marshall a copy of his first gold record.

If he could only finish that damn demo tape . . .

Diamond walked into Marshall's office with a dream in his head and the prize in his eyes. Marshall had already sat down behind his desk.

"What up?"

"Sit down, Diamond."

"Oh, I know this is going to be good."

Marshall hauled out a thick black ledger. Flipping it open to a section marked "Diamond," he took out reading glasses from his shirt pocket and peered through them at the figures.

"Look, Marshall, I know I've been promising to catch up on my account—"

"Diamond, you got to face the facts, man. You just can't afford this."

"Look, Marshall, I just finished my demo and I . . ."

"That's what you said when you cut your last demo, remember?"

"What are you saying? That I don't have what it takes?"

"I know you've got the goods. Why do you think I've been carrying you for this long? But there comes a point where I gotta just say no."

"C'mon man, I'm almost there."

Marshall leaned forward, his face all business. "Look, Diamond. I get kids coming in here and cutting a whole CD in the time it takes you to do one demo track."

"I'm not just putting any ole junk together. You know that."

"Yeah. But unfortunately, I don't sell albums, I sell studio time. That's how I pay the rent."

"I'm just asking you to carry me for another couple of sessions, Marshall, that's all."

Marshall shook his head. "I've been through this a lot of times, with a lot of people, and I'm gonna tell you how it goes. I let someone like yourself record here on account, and then after some time, some tracks are put down and I still won't see a dime. But I think to myself, if I pull the plug now, I'll never see the money or the person again. So I let them record some more, hoping that they'll get things done and then they'll be able to pay me. But time goes by, and pretty soon you're into me for so much scratch that I'm afraid to cut you off—and it just keeps on going. And in the end, I still never see a dime." Marshall paused and peered. "It ain't nothing personal, Diamond—it's just time."

Diamond slowly rose and left Marshall's office.

Returning to the studio, Diamond heard his music pumping out the loudspeaker, but Baz was nowhere in sight. Adjusting a few levels, Diamond left the recording booth and walked down the studio hall toward the bathrooms.

Opening the door, he saw Baz stooped over the sink, snorting coke through a rolled bill off of the dark colored tile. Baz spun around quickly at the sound of the door, like a thief caught red-handed. Grinning sheepishly, he tried to stammer an explanation. "Yo, D, I'm just havin' a little fun, you know?"

"No wonder you can't hear worth shit Baz—you're too fucking wasted all the time!"

"It ain't like that D!"

"Look, don't lay that on me Baz. You're fired. I ain't working with you anymore." Diamond said.

"Fired? How you gonna fire me if you ain't even paid me yet?"

"You'll get your money. Now get the fuck out of here," Diamond yelled, pointing toward the door.

Baz scoffed, pushing past Diamond on out of the studio. Diamond ran his hands over his head, his mind a whirl. Looking down at the traces of white powder on the counter, he became even more enraged. Not only was he kicked out of the studio, the tracks he did manage to lay down were all jumbled and mixed poorly by an idiot cokehead.

Overcome by anger, he balled up his hands, looking for something, anything, to hit. As he did, he caught his reflection in the mirror. He studied the hard face that looked back at him, at eyes that have seen too much pain and hardship, at fists that have taken part in their fair share of violence. For a second, Diamond wanted to lash out against himself, to rail against himself and the life he was living.

Everything was beginning to unravel. He felt alone, like every relationship he had was tenuous, bordering on the brink of collapse. Tamara's pregnancy had thrown him a curve he had no idea how to handle. Baz just seemed to drag him down. His mysterious and gruff father just turned up out of the blue. And then, Michael's crazy ideas and violent temper were sure to get them in real deep trouble—or worse—sooner than later.

Diamond took a deep breath, trying to calm his frazzled nerves. Closing his eyes, he exhaled, then looked again at his reflection. Not being able to stop himself, he smashed the mirror with his fist, shattering the glass, leaving broken cobwebbed fragments across its surface.

With a screech of rubber, Gage pulled up to the recording studio in his Bronco. Leaping out of the sports utility vehicle, he glided up to and through the studio's front door. Baz was in the lobby, packing up his.

"Yo, where's Diamond?"

"Your homeboy is tripping man!" Baz cried. "Thinks he can fire my ass, and he hasn't even paid me in weeks! I ain't with that shit."

"'Bout time he fired your sorry ass," Gage laughed.

Baz stuffed the rest of his gear into the bag and stormed out of the studio in a huff. Gage watched him waddle out the door, then turned around as Diamond came down the hall, his hand wrapped in a bundle of bloody toilet tissue.

"What are you doing here?"

Gage was taken aback by Diamond's blunt manner. "I ain't no blowhead flunkie like Baz—this is your homey, Gage."

"Yeah, yeah, right. What up, Gage?"

"Am I your manager, or what?" Gage said, opening his arms and grinning broadly. Apparently all was forgiven from their altercation at the club.

Diamond paused for a beat. With everything that was happening in his life and his career, could it get any worse than having Gage as his manager? "Yeah, sure," he replied.

Gage laughed. "Dog, you gonna be large, I promise you that!"

"Marshall pulled the plug on me. No more studio time until I come up with the cash."

"Then I guess I got here just in time."

"Time for what?"

"I told you it was time to get out of the minors and move up to the major league."

Gage reached into his coat pocket and pulled out a thick worn envelope with a rubber band around it. Flipping it open, Diamond saw that the envelope was stuffed full of crisp one-hundred dollar bills, which Gage riffled in front of Diamond's widening eyes.

"Twenty thousand dollars dog!" Gage shouted. "Are you ready to play?"

"How did you get that much money?" Diamond asked slack-jawed.

"Never mind that—you ready to play?"

Diamond stared at the money intently. The heady smell of the fresh bills was intoxicating. Diamond could see the potential of all that money— it was as if Gage held the key to his future right there in that yellowed envelope. Twenty thousand dollars could do a lot. No more problems with Marshall; Diamond could pay for studio time way in advance. That would give him the time and space he needed to really make his tracks smoke. Maybe he could hire a professional to help him mix the tunes. And forget about a demo tape. He would have enough capital to release his own CDs and have them distributed throughout the area. He would make sure Mr. White got a hold of one, too. That way a large company might back Diamond up on his next release.

Diamond knew that it only took one mega-hit for an independent label to hit the big time. With Gage's cash, their label might be the next Death Row Records. Diamond's eyes were glued to the cash. He began to wonder whose pockets it came from. Or from which hands it was ripped out of.

Gage saw the shadow pass in front of Diamond's eyes.

"What's wrong, dog? Don't you want to be no ghetto supastar no more?" he asked, fanning the bills in Diamond's face.

"I want to know who you killed to get that money," Diamond replied.

Gage slowly extended his palm toward Diamond, the money spread wide in his hand. "When Jesus healed the blind man, did the man ask Jesus how he did it?"

"You ain't Jesus. And I certainly ain't blind." They both broke into wide, smiling grins. Diamond fidgeted with his damaged hand, almost having to keep it from reaching out and snatching the cash. The allure of the money in front of him was irresistible; its pull was powerful and compelling. And Gage knew it.

"What's it gonna be, D? My arm is getting tired holding this wad up."

Diamond reached out with his bloodied hand and grabbed the envelope.

"You the man." Gage smiled as they made it down the hall toward Marshall's office.

The room swayed with young brothers and sisters, all to the steady beat put out by a young rapper on stage. Every Thursday night the Hip Hop Emporium was wall-to-wall bodies, slamming, dancing, yelling, and singing. People would come into the city from miles around, just to hear the latest and bravest live, in person, because every Thursday the club turned the mic over to the crowd.

Lists were filled of young talent waiting to strut their stuff in front of the jiving masses. If they had flavor, they were hailed. If they were stale or rapped like chumps, the crowd let them know. Records spun and scratched, the bass rocked the room as much as the jumping feet. Open Mike Nite at the Hip Hop Emporium was a glorious thing indeed.

It was business as usual this Thursday night, as a kid named Johnny Ray was rapping to the throng of dancers below the stage. Wearing loose athletic gear and a red baseball cap turned askew, Johnny Ray was making the joint jump. "Give me an aaaaay yo!" he screamed at the throng.

"Aaaay yo!" the crowd answered as one in a deafening shout. Response after response, Johnny Ray made sure the crowd kept grooving to the funky beat.

Outside the club, Gage and Diamond walked past the line at the front door. At least forty people were waiting to get in. Those closest to the front of the line were craning their heads over the bouncers meaty shoulders, desperate to get a peek at what was going on inside. Gage and Diamond turned the corner and made their way to the back entrance to the club. A few people were waiting there as well, held back by another muscular bouncer in a skin-tight T-shirt. As they approached the door, the bouncer greeted them like celebrities, ordering a few milling people out of their way so they could enter.

"What up Gage?" asked the bouncer eagerly as the two made their way through.

"How you doing my brother?" replied Gage, slapping the bouncer's hand. Diamond noticed some green passing between their palms.

"I'm good, I'm good," said the bouncer with a knowing wink. He turned to Diamond. "So, you gonna rap tonight?" he asked him.

"Thinking about it," said Diamond.

Gage punched Diamond lightly on the arm. "Yo, he's gonna bring the house down tonight!"

"Ain't that what they all say?" the guard laughed, and ushered them into the club. Diamond led the way to the backstage area where several other rappers were hanging out, listening to Johnny Ray finish up. A few were waiting their turn at the mic, but when they saw Diamond, they made way for him with a deferential respect.

Diamond nodded back, taking a peek at the crowd from the wings. He had never seen the place so packed before. Girls were mugging the stage, begging Johnny Ray for his number, a piece of clothing, anything they could take home as a souvenir. People were dancing like mad, grinding and stomping.

As Johnny Ray finished with a flourish, the MC took the stage. Seeing Diamond waiting on the side, he shouted to the crowd, "Yo that was Johnny Ray, y'all. Give it up!" The crowd went wild with applause and calls. "And now, straight outta the streets of Brooklyn . . . y'all know him and love him . . . a young veteran of the

Emporium . . . he's big, he's bad, like a dog gone mad, here is Diamond St. James!"

The crowd whooped in enthusiasm. Diamond had only rapped at Open Mic Nite three times before, but each time, he had clearly blown all the other rappers away. He was the house favorite, and the mob let him know it.

Gage led Diamond to the mic like Don King would lead a fighter to a championship bout, pointing and yelling. The DJ blasted out a heavy beat as Diamond grabbed the mic.

And then he began to rhyme.

Few rap artists completely mesmerize a crowd as they spin their words. Few can drive them wild with their lyrical gymnastics, and force feet to move to a contagious beat. Diamond was one of the few, and as he rapped, the Hip Hop Emporium went hysterical. He had the women swooning and men literally jumping up and down with wild abandon. Diamond's rhymes were at once poignant, brilliant, and awesome. He had everyone singing the chorus along with him. Kids were having the time of their lives on the dance floor, and it was clear that once again, Diamond was king of Open Mic Nite.

After the song finished, the thunderous applause and enthusiastic catcalls went on for five minutes. Diamond, his face beaming under the bright lights, thanked the crowd, slapped fives with people near the stage, and was almost carried into the crowd like a hero being welcomed home. Girls were clutching at his hands, enraptured by the handsome rapper. Diamond quickly ran off-stage, where Gage was standing with open arms.

"Yo, D, you know you just ripped it, right?" Gage said. Several other rappers, including Johnny Ray, nodded in agreement, congratulating Diamond.

Diamond tried to act nonchalant. "It's cool," he replied. He couldn't suppress his smile, though.

Gage threw an arm around his shoulder and led him toward the backstage area. "Dog, you know that joint was off the hook! Yo, that rhyme was hot. We gotta lay that on the album."

Diamond could still hear the crowd cheering as the MC tried to quiet them down for the next act. With their roar in his ears, Diamond could actually see the future gleaming brightly in front of him. For the first time, the possibility of success seemed more than just a dream. He could almost taste it.

Diamond lay sleeping in bed, exhausted from the night before. He had stayed at the club until dawn, dancing and talking with several beautiful ladies. When he finally returned to the apartment, he was drunk, tired, but happy. It was the afternoon already, and still, Diamond was dead to the world. Until the silence of the apartment was shattered by thumping bass, a wailing hip hop groove, and loud beats from the living room speakers. Diamond shot up in his bed in shock. "What the fuck?" he asked his bedroom walls, rubbing his bleary eyes.

The music sounded familiar to Diamond, but he was still too disoriented to recognize it. Suddenly, he recognized that it was his own voice rapping. Pulling on a pair of sweatpants, Diamond staggered his way out of his bedroom.

The stereo was on, but no one was in the living room. Diamond took a peek into the kitchen, where he saw Cliff, standing over the stove, about to fry up some eggs and bacon.

"Hey I was trying to get some sleep."

"You know what time it is?" Cliff asked condescendingly, looking at his watch. Diamond shook his head, not caring, trying to wipe the sleep from his eyes. "It's just after two o'clock."

Cliff turned from the stove and took two plates out of the cupboard. Setting them out on the kitchen table, he motioned for Diamond to sit as he returned to the stove. "Well, go on, sit and eat something," he said, stirring the eggs vigorously in the pan.

Diamond plunked himself down at the table as Cliff came over with a sizzling frying pan. "I've made the bacon extra crispy," said Cliff, placing four very charred strips on Diamond's plate.

Diamond looked at the pathetic pieces of bacon, then back up at Cliff, who was smiling at him. *He might be a musician, but he certainly ain't no cook,* Diamond thought, shaking his head. "Thanks," he said. "It's just the way I like it."

"Thought so," said Cliff, and went back to the stove for eggs. When both plates were loaded with food, Cliff sat down and began to dig in. He looked up, his face full of eggs, and noticed Diamond hadn't even touched his breakfast yet.

"What's wrong?" asked Cliff, chewing thoughtfully.

"Nothing, nothing," Diamond replied. Leaning back, he cocked his head to one side, listening to his song, which was still blasting out of the stereo speakers. "You haven't said anything about my demo yet. What do you think?" said Diamond.

Cliff swallowed slowly, then washed the eggs down with a long hearty slurp of coffee. Diamond was beside himself in anticipation, wanting to know what his father, the musician, thought of his tunes.

"It's alright," said Cliff, shrugging his shoulders and lifting up his fork again.

"Alright? That's it? It's damn hot is what it is, right?" said Diamond.

"You asked me for my opinion, and I gave it to you."

"What's wrong with it?"

Cliff put down his fork. "Well, it just sounds like all the other rap I hear on the radio all the time, that's all."

"Naw, naw, man. This sound is fresh!"

"Maybe I'm the wrong person to ask," said Cliff, rising to clear his dishes.

Diamond interrupted him, placing a hand on Cliff's arm. "Don't go all soft on me now, bro. For real, what's wrong with my sound?"

Cliff paused. "Well, it sounds too processed, for one thing. There's no feel to it; you know what I'm saying? There's no bottom—your bass sounds too compressed. You're pushing the sound, but it's got no bite."

"Aw, shit," said Diamond dejectedly.

Cliff walked over to the sink, turned the faucet on, and began to wash his dish.

"I'll tell you what the problem is. You kids are growing up on preproccessed, digitized, homogenized, computer-enhanced, synthesized music. You think that your Yamaha keyboard samplers sound like a real piano."

"I know what a real piano sounds like."

Diamond was stunned by Cliff's critique. Although not spiteful, the words still stung. Why, just last night, there were tons of people who didn't mind the sound one bit. But then again, his father was a musician and knew a lot more about sound, music theory, and studio recording than Diamond did.

"You may know what a piano sounds like, but you gotta know how to use its sound. C'mon, I'll prove it," said Cliff, who turned off the water and headed toward Diamond's bedroom. Diamond quickly got up and followed.

When he entered Diamond's room, Cliff walked right over to the Yamaha keyboard and flipped the power on. He motioned for Diamond to sit.

"Go ahead," he said, "play something for me."

Diamond shrugged but sat down, complying with his father's request. He fiddled around with the settings, then depressed a few keys. The notes came out sounding like the deep, vibrant tones of a Hammond organ. Cycling through a few more of the preprogrammed sounds, Diamond finally got the sound he was looking for. As he played a few notes, the rich timbre of a grand piano filled the room.

"Yeah that's it," Cliff sighed, "I want to hear that hunk of plastic sound like a real instrument."

Diamond's fingers danced across the keyboard, playing a complex yet harmonious classical piece. The music seemed to envelop him as he played. Cliff was impressed by his son's playing technique and wondered where he picked it up from.

Just as he was about to praise Diamond for his sound, steady style, Diamond threw in a fancy improvised glissando, winking at Cliff just to make a point. Even a hip hopper could appreciate the classics.

Cliff smiled. "Not bad, not bad at all. You know I used to play that very same song for you when you were a baby."

Diamond paused slightly, then continued playing. "I know," he said, without looking up.

There was a strange silence between them as Diamond played on, the music swelling to a crescendo. Just as he finished the piece, Cliff grabbed Diamond by the arm, tugging at his elbow.

"Come on, let's go. I want to take you somewhere."

"Where are we going?" asked Diamond.

"You'll see. Now it's my turn," Cliff said as he led Diamond out the apartment door.

The Trump Tower in midtown Manhattan is an awesome sight. Every year, thousands upon thousands of tourists walk through its magnificent marbled lobby, admiring its sleek copper waterfalls and the impressive glass display windows filled with exotic gifts and expensive jewelry. They wander the gigantic concourse lined with cafés and shops. Some tourists have even caught a glimpse of Trump himself, hurrying out of the lobby with his entourage, on his way to buy another large chunk of the city.

From the outside, Trump Tower is a magnificent edifice of staggered smoked glass, with lush greenery hanging heavily from its terraces. This theme is picked up in the lobby, where spectacular vines and gardens wind their way across the palatial hall. But the centerpiece of the lobby, arranged on a slightly raised dais and surrounded by tropical flower arrangements and Grecian urns, is a large, ivory white grand piano.

Diamond and Cliff stood in the middle of the lobby, feeling out of place amid the buzzing throng of tourists and business people, scurrying in and out of the building in their crisp Armani suits. The traffic out on Fifth Avenue was choked with people shopping, sightseeing, and getting back to work like so many drones, as if they were ants returning to the farm.

"Well?" Diamond said. "Are we just gonna stare at it all day or did you have something special in mind?"

Cliff shot Diamond a look, and then approached the piano in the middle of the lobby. It was cordoned off by red velvet ropes, but Cliff easily stepped over the barrier with his lanky legs and then sat down at the piano, adjusting the seat slightly as he did.

From the very first note he played, Cliff commanded attention. The full sound of the grand piano seemed to resonate off the marble walls, overflowing the lobby with symphonic splendor. Cliff began softly, playing a classical song, but soon his playing built up into a veritable tidal wave of melodious sound. A few people stopped and moved closer to the dais, taken in by the music, trying to see who was playing the piano with so much skill.

Cliff's fingers danced and leaped like a chorus line as he played, his eyes closed, his body swaying with the sweet rhythms. It was Diamond's turn to be impressed, as Cliff mesmerized the onlookers. Building, Cliff began to play faster, the notes tumbling down much like the waterfall behind him. He seemed to elevate the piece, taking it beyond the boundaries of where it was supposed to go, making the music seem alive. The crowd was stunned and clapped lightly as Cliff began to improvise with the piece, adding jazzy flourishes and runs, warming the stoic classical song up a little bit.

And soon, it became hot. Cliff banged out the notes like a man possessed, and the sublime Trump Tower lobby became a honky-tonk juke joint. People laughed and danced as Cliff played, his music a presence of its own. Cliff made the piano jump and shake, and Diamond was loving it.

As Cliff continued to play, a thought nagged at the corner of Diamond's mind, just out of reach. Something was familiar to him about the music Cliff was playing. Sure, it was a fusion of classical and jazz, but underneath it all was a steady rhythm, a pulse of a beat that got Diamond's toes tapping.

As Cliff played, Diamond closed his eyes. A hip-hop groove surfaced from the recesses of his brain. He could almost hear synthesized drumbeats underneath the music Cliff was playing, turning the song into an electric mix of rap and jazz. As Diamond let his ears fill with the sound, a thought struck him like a thunderbolt, making his heart beat faster and the hairs stand up on the back of his neck.

Diamond sat in the soundproof booth, rapping happily to the music. Behind the glass, in the control room, Cliff sat behind the mixing board, nodding his head in time with the groove. Marshall sat beside Cliff, smiling, caught up with Diamond's enthusiastic rhymes as he tweaked the levels and adjusted volumes.

Gage, who sat in the corner of the control room, crowed loudly. "Yo, now listen to my homey heat up those tracks!"

"He certainly is something else," replied Marshall, folding his big hands across his chest.

"Just you wait," said Cliff, "things are about to get a little hotter." As Diamond finished the song, Cliff walked out of the booth toward the lobby. He returned seconds later with a stooped old man with a pork-pie hat, a thin weathered tie, and beat-up gig bag. "Gentlemen, I'd like you to meet my friend, Lips."

Diamond entered the room as Gage and Marshall said hello to this strange man. He seemed like he was from another era—the Depression, perhaps—and his voice, which was like a low, raspy cough, only added to his mystique.

"Yo Cliff," said Diamond. "Is this the man?"

"He sure is. Lips, I'd like you to meet my son, Diamond."

"Pleasure," croaked Lips.

"You ready to get it on?" asked Diamond.

"I've been ready since the day I was born, son," replied Lips, as he took a beat-up old trumpet out of his gig bag. Diamond wondered if the old man would be able to get a sound out of the battered instrument as Lips fingered the levers and softened the reed.

Lips crossed into the studio and sat on a stool. Removing his hat gingerly and placing it on a stand, he blew a few notes into the trumpet. Diamond realized that rather than being decrepit the instrument had aged like a fine wine, its sound resonant and true. Marshall adjusted a few levels and then motioned for Lips to play.

And play he did. From the first puff of his cheeks to the last piercing lick, Lips's music crackled and hummed. Playing over Diamond's hiphop funk, Lips's jazz trumpet took the music to a higher level, infusing it with sleek style and a unique rhythm. Diamond had never heard anything like it before. Even Marshall was shaking his head in amazement, both at the old man's agility and the fresh new sound he was creating.

As Lips blew a final, wavering note over the track, the control room burst into eager applause.

Wiping his mouth, Lips bowed his head in appreciation.

"You, you're the bomb," Gage called out.

"I told you he was the best," said Cliff.

Lips wasn't phased a bit by the open adoration. "I'd like to try that one more time. I just ain't hearing it yet."

Diamond looked over at Marshall, shrugging his shoulders. "Do what the man says," he stated, as Marshall cued up the track again.

Diamond was beyond impressed—he was ecstatic. For the first time, his music seemed right. With the driving beat of the hip-hop groove and the smoky accents of jazz, Diamond knew he had the sound.

Turning to Gage, Diamond spoke, completely overwhelmed. "Yo, dog, is this for real?"

"It's good, D, it's all good. We the baddest motherfucking record producers in Brooklyn!" Gage slapped fives with Diamond, Cliff, and Marshall. Oblivious to the all the gushing emotion in the control room, Lips played on, searing the track with his signature horn playing.

"Gage's cell phone suddenly began to ring from the inside pocket of his Tommy Hilfiger jacket. Whipping it out, he quickly answered the call.

"Yeah, wassup? Hey, Mr. B, how's it hangin'? I'm fine . . . no I ain't been hiding. I'm working with my boy Diamond right now . . . Naw, man, I'm never too busy for you, Mr. B. I'll be right there."

Gage flipped his phone off and crammed it back

into his jacket pocket as Diamond, who heard the conversation, looked over in concern.

"Yo, D, I'm outta here," said Gage, putting on his shades.

Diamond scowled. "Fuck Mr. B, Gage. You don't got to be doing that shit anymore. You're a record producer now, you even said it for yourself."

"Dog, the way you been spending the money, I'm gonna have to make another withdrawal. Yo, I got to produce in order to be a producer, you know what I'm saying?" replied Gage nonchalantly.

"I'll go with you," said Diamond.

"Naw, man, it's no big thing," said Gage, already making his way out of the studio.

"Alright, then, I'll catch up with you later." Diamond turned back to the sound board, and with the slightest feeling of trepidation, focused on his music.

Mr. B sat in his favorite leather chair in the back room of his bar, which was located on a dark street just on the edge of town. It wasn't going well for Mr. B tonight—he was already down a few grand, and they had only been playing poker for just over an hour. Hand after hand, his straights were beaten by flushes, his high pairs with three of a kinds. As the chips dwindled in front of him, Mr. B's sour mood just turned ugly. His cronies, laughing and getting richer at his expense, weren't helping any.

"Yo, Mr. B. Maybe that's enough for one night,

eh? I don't think I want to see you without a shirt on," chuckled Tin.

"Yo, man, stop cutting the boss and start cutting the cards," said Crusher threateningly, slamming his beefy hand down on the green felt table, making the ante pot jump.

JT cut the cards and handed them to Slick, who called out seven-card stud and began to deal them out. Mr. B was trying to will a winning hand out of the deck, but when the cards landed in front of him—a three and a six, with a nine as his down card—he let out a frustrated sigh.

"Fucking horse shit," Mr. B mumbled, as he looked around at the other players' cards.

JT had an ace-king up. Crusher had a pair of sevens. And Tyrone, leaning back in his seat smugly, was showing two queens. "That's what they call the Siegfried and Roy hand in Vegas, " he chuckled, making Mr. B fume even more.

Just then, Gage walked through the door, striding boldly up to the table. "Not your night, huh, Mr. B?" he asked, noting the conspicuous absence of chips in his pile as compared to the abundance of the others around the table.

"Every night's my night," replied Mr. B, flipping his cards over. "I fold. Gage, follow me to the bar. We have business to discuss," he said, rising from the table.

The two made their way over to the long cedar bar while the game continued. Mr. B grabbed two highball glasses and filled them with ice and top-shelf bourbon. Handing Gage a glass, Mr. B took a long sip, studying him intently.

Gage began to feel uncomfortable. "Yo, what's up?" he asked.

"I want you to pick up a package uptown for me," Mr. B said after a pause.

"Shit, is that all? No problem, Mr. B, I'll just pop by and . . ."

"Watch your back," Mr. B interrupted, his tone darkening considerably. "You heard that Hollis got jacked?"

"Yeah, what of it?"

"He had twenty thousand of mine."

"Hollis? But he don't even work for you."

Mr. B put down his drink and began to rub his hands together. "Let's just say we were doing a little business transaction. I think whoever did this knew that Hollis was loaded. I'm thinking it might be one of Teddy's boys," he said, still watching Gage closely. Gage kept a poker face, waiting to see where Mr. B was going with this.

After a few moments, Mr. B seemed to let his guard down. "That was the problem with Hollis," he finally continued, "he couldn't keep his mouth shut. So that's why I'm telling you—watch yourself. You're a good kid, Gage." Mr. B put a firm hand on Gage's shoulder, almost a little too firm.

And with that, he turned back to his card game, leaving Gage at the bar with his drink.

Diamond and Gage were back at the Hip Hop Emporium, sitting back with some beers, taking in the scene around them. It was a little mellower tonight than Open Mic Nite, but not by much. People swirled on the dance floor as the music kicked out of the sound system like an angry mule. There were gorgeous women everywhere.

Gage watched one woman, who wore just a tank top and silk trousers, as she sauntered up to the bar.

"So, D," he said, turning his attention to another beauty across the room, "you've been in the studio for half a month, now. When are the tracks going to be finished?"

"Two more days," answered Diamond. "Then all we have to do is mix it down to the master." For two weeks, Diamond never left the studio. With the help of his father, who enlisted several excellent jazz musicians to join them in the studio, the sessions were absolute dynamite. Cliff had been more than helpful, giving tips on arranging some songs, suggesting some killer breaks, even lending his recording expertise to the tracks. The results were shaping up to be one hell of a demo.

Most of all, Diamond enjoyed watching his father sit in on the sessions. Cliff would be a frantic perfectionist in the control booth, but once he sat down behind the piano, it was as if he was a different man. His uptight manner was replaced by an easygoing attitude as he joked and jammed with his fellow musicians. The banter between them was often hilarious, and Diamond soon found out he could pick up a few tips on the industry just by listening to the old timers talk.

"You are going to be so large, you know what I'm saying?" said Gage, snapping Diamond out of his reverie. He couldn't help but grin like a small kid in a candy store.

"It's good, man, it's all good," he replied, leaning back and placing his hands behind his head like a man who had it made.

Just then, Baz stumbled up to their table, obviously wasted. His face was flashed with sweat, and his eyes darted around maniacally. He kept glancing behind him, seemingly paranoid that he was being followed.

Baz ground his teeth when he talked. "Yo, D, wassup?"

Diamond knew Baz was just coming from the restrooms, where more likely than not, he had snorted a few too many lines of blow. "I'm good, Baz, what's up with you?"

"I'm good too," Baz replied, giggling. "Gage, my man, what you been doing?"

"Just hanging," said Gage, a little put out by this buffoon and wondering just what the hell Baz wanted.

Baz sniffed loudly a few times while glancing around him. "I hear you're recording an album," he said to Diamond.

"Yeah, that's right. What of it?"

"That must be costing you a shitload of money, huh?" Diamond didn't respond, so Baz continued, wiping his palms on his pants. "It's funny how when you finish, you forget all about your boy Baz."

"You got paid," Diamond said bluntly.

"That's right, I got paid," said Baz, getting angry now. "I got paid and then I got kicked out right on my ass."

Gage stood up, putting his face tight in Baz's

sweaty mug. "Why don't you just bounce your ass outta here, too, man," he threatened.

Baz backed down, shooting Diamond a nasty look. "Alright, later," he said, turning to push through the crowd. As Diamond and Gage sat back down again, laughing at him, Baz made his way toward the payphones in the back of the club.

"I'll show those niggas who they messin' with," he said to no one in particular, as he dropped a quarter into the slot. On the other side of town, the phone rang in Mr. B's backroom office. Crusher picked it up.

"Hello."

"Hey, put Mr. B on the line," Baz said anxiously.

"Who is this?" asked Crusher.

Baz, in a cocaine-induced fury, lost his patience and yelled into the phone. "If Mr. B wants to know who did Hollis, tell him to pick up the fucking phone. Right now!"

Meanwhile, Diamond sucked back the rest of his beer and stood up. "I'm outta here," he said. "I gotta go back to the studio to finish up some tracks."

Gage was watching a girl who danced seductively a few feet away, her eyes locked on his. "Yeah, whatever, cool. I'll catch up with you later on," he said, no longer really listening.

"Go easy on her, Gage. She looks like she has some class," Diamond joked. Gage just waved him away, smiling at the girl and motioning for her to join him at the table.

BLUE ANGEL
(NO FORWARDS)

Cliff sat in the empty studio, playing the piano. It was a soft, haunting, melodic song that seemed to bring back memories for him. As Diamond sat and watched his father, he noticed how his face seemed calm, almost thoughtful. As the song ended, Diamond could not help but feel moved.

"That was beautiful, man," Diamond said, startling Cliff.

"I wrote that for your mother when I first met her," he replied quietly.

"Why didn't you record any of your own music?" Diamond asked.

"Wasn't that easy. Studio time was expensive. You couldn't get a record deal if your life depended on it. The white cats Uptown decided what the people wanted to listen to. And I wasn't it," Cliff said with a note of regret in his voice.

"That's all wrong, man!" Diamond exclaimed.

"I look around and I don't see how anything has changed though," Cliff replied. "You have that same look of determination in your eyes that

I had when I was your age. And it's still the white cats Uptown calling the shots."

Diamond set his chin firmly. "Yeah, well, I'm not letting anyone stop me."

Cliff laughed, shaking his head. "That's what I used to think."

"I don't mean to disrespect you or nothing, Cliff, but I think if you had just stayed off the bottle, you would've made it. And I'm not saying that to be judgmental, you know what I'm saying?"

Cliff swiveled around on his stool to face Diamond. Looking up and pointing at his chest, he said, "I'm gonna tell you something, son. It wasn't the drinking that brought me down. When I was a kid, all I wanted to do was play music. It's all that I thought about, and pretty much all that I did. But as time went on, and as I became older and wiser, I started to realize that I wasn't going to be the next Duke Ellington, or the greatest since Charlie Parker. Call it fate, call it luck, call it destiny. But it just wasn't going to happen for me."

Diamond opened his mouth to protest, but Cliff cut him off. "Look, I wasn't the first talented musician to go unnoticed, and I'm sure as hell not going to be the last. If it was that easy, nobody would be driving cabs, or stacking shelves, or mopping floors like your mother, or doing God knows what while they waited endlessly for their big break. Mine just didn't come, that's all," Cliff said, hanging his head slightly.

"And when I stopped hoping," Cliff picked up after a slight pause, "when I stopped believing in myself and my ability . . . that's when I got to drinking. I wish I could blame the bottle. That would have at least given me a reason to call it quits. But I would just be lying to myself. In the end, I just couldn't face being a failure."

A long silence ensued as Cliff's words sunk in. Diamond then perked up. "But it ain't over, not just yet. When this album comes out, and the kids check out who is playing all this sweet jazz, they're gonna be saying, 'Cliff St. James is the bomb.' "

"You just don't get it, do you, son? That doesn't matter to me anymore. Music and money and fame aren't everything, you know. I had a wife, and a child, and I let them go because I thought all that was more important. That's what brought me down, son—do you understand what I'm saying?"

Diamond could see Cliff's eyes moisten as his father pleaded with him. Only now did he see his father's true regret, and though it hurt Diamond to think about how his father had abandoned his mother and him, he could see the pain and torture it brought Cliff to think about how his life could have been had he remained with them all these years. Rather than feeling sorry for his father, Diamond felt a deep respect for a man who had the courage to forge ahead with a dream, and to realize the mistakes he had made in life.

After a moment, Diamond turned to go. "I gotta go take care of some business. I'll be back in about an hour, okay?" he said.

"You know I'm not going anywhere," replied Cliff, turning back to the piano.

As Diamond walked out the door, he heard his father's voice quietly speaking behind him. "Thanks," Cliff said.

Diamond turned around in the doorway. "For what?"

"For being my son."

Diamond stared at his father, the two sharing a knowing look. Nothing more needed to be said.

Meanwhile, Gage was sitting at the same table at the Hip Hop Emporium, with the fine woman he had been making time with perched in his lap. She was kissing Gage's neck, thrusting her chest into his face while Gage remained nonchalant, playing it cool. As he was about to kiss her back, his cell phone rang, interrupting the moment.

"Just a moment, sugar," Gage said, as the girl got off him and sat in the chair, pouting playfully. "Yo wassup?" Gage said into his phone. "Hey, Mr. B, I was just . . . Now? . . . Alright, I'll be there in five."

Gage put the phone back into his jacket, shaking his head regretfully. "Damn! Look," he said turning to the girl, "what did you say your name was?"

"Leronda," the girl responded, a little put out.

"Well, Leronda, I gotta fly. Why don't you give me your number and I'll call you later, okay, baby?"

Leronda flashed him a stern look, giving him

attitude. "You better call if I be giving you my number, 'cause I just don't give it out to anybody."

Gage smiled, turning up the charm. "Well, baby, I'm not just anybody. I'm a superstar," he said giving her a kiss and then rising to go.

Tamara lay sleeping in bed. She had finally drifted off after tossing and turning for hours. Her life was turned upside down, and her future seemed rocky. She still wasn't sure what she was going to do about the baby, and she hadn't heard from Diamond in days. She was ready to just cut him out of her life, and although she was determined to make the best of the situation, she missed Diamond's soothing presence, his sage advice, and most of all, his strong arms holding her tight.

A loud thud at her window jarred Tamara awake. Glancing sleepily over at the alarm clock, she saw it was three A.M. She cursed as she got out of bed to see who was there.

It was Diamond.

Tamara shook her head in annoyance. If Diamond wanted to talk, why didn't he come over a few days ago? And during daylight hours, for goodness sake.

"What the hell are you doing here, Diamond?" she fumed once she had snuck him back into her room.

"Look, baby, can't we just talk?"

Tamara crossed her hands over her breasts, giving him a cold stare. "I'm done talking to you," she replied.

"C'mon, baby, don't be playing like this," Diamond begged good-naturedly.

Tamara held her ground. "I'm not playing at anything, Diamond. I'm the one who's pregnant, remember?"

"That's why I'm over here. I've done some thinking, and I don't want to lose you over this," he said.

"What exactly do you mean when you say 'this'?"

"You know what I'm saying," Diamond replied with a grin, nodding toward her stomach.

"No, I don't know what you're saying."

"What I'm saying is that I love you, Tamara, and I want to have this baby with you."

"But two weeks ago you didn't want to have anything to do with the baby. Why the concern now?" Tamara spat.

Diamond placed his hands gently on Tamara's forearms. "When you first told me you were pregnant, the first thing that came to my mind was to run. I admit it. I think it's just the first reaction any guy might have. But then I remembered my own father walking out on me and my mom. I was afraid that if I said I was gonna be there for you, I wouldn't be able to stay true to my word, and I'd end up taking off anyway."

Tamara scowled. "So what makes you come back now?"

"Because I'm not my father. And I'm not going to make the same mistakes that he made," Diamond said earnestly, drawing her closer to him.

Tamara looked into Diamond's eyes and saw

that he meant what he said. Lightening a little, she said, "You sure are a changed man."

Diamond grinned. "I want you to listen to something."

He let go of her and walked quickly over to the stereo, flipping on the cassette deck. From his pocket, he took out a black tape and slid it in the stereo. "This is gonna be on my album. I wanted you to be the first to hear it."

With that, Diamond pressed PLAY, watching Tamara's reaction closely. The song kicked in, but not loud enough to wake Ms. Lewis, who was sleeping in the next room, with a soulful jazz riff on the piano, making Tamara think of smoke-filled bars and cheap whiskey. It was beautiful, lively yet elegant. Soon, a cool hip-hop groove made its presence known, and the room filled with the syncopated beats and rhythms of Diamond's music. Tamara couldn't help but sway to the tune.

Then Diamond's voice came on, a rich baritone over the music. His lyrics were heartfelt and uplifting as he rapped about life in the ghetto, how every brother deserves his chance. Diamond rapped about love and faith, and about sticking together.

Impressed, Tamara beamed at him. "That's something else, Diamond," she lauded, as Diamond moved over to her and planted a warm kiss on her forehead. "I've never heard anything like it—it's awesome."

"That's my new sound, sugar," replied Diamond. "When this little tape hits the radio, our lives are gonna change. Forever." The two hugged each other tightly in the faint dawn light.

MURDER THEM
(NO FORWARDS)

Having completed its swing, the heavy object, laden with metal, pulled back slightly before launching forward once again. A sickening crunch ensued as the metal's sharp edges tore away at flesh, breaking bone. The object was Mr. B's fist, full of gaudy jeweled rings. The flesh was Gage's, who bled profusely from his broken nose, his face battered and pulpy.

Mr. B stepped back from his handiwork, wiping off his fist with a cotton handkerchief. Gage slumped forward as Tyrone and JT jerked him on his feet again.

"I thought you were smarter than this Gage," said Mr. B condescendingly. "First you fuck up by stealing my money." Mr. B nodded toward Crusher, who stepped forward to deliver a punishing blow to Gage's ribcage. "And now," Mr. B continued, "you take a beating instead of just owning up to it."

Crusher bitch-slapped Gage, leaving his cheek stinging as his neck snapped backward. As Crusher got ready to swing again, Mr. B stopped him. Gage was trying to mutter something about Hollis between broken teeth and swollen split lips.

Mr. B stepped closer to Gage, putting his face right up against Gage's. "I really don't give a fuck what you did to Hollis. He was a worthless piece of shit, anyway. All I am interested in is my money, Gage."

Gage's bruised eyes rolled back. "I . . . don't have it," he gasped in pain.

"Then where the fuck is it?" Mr. B screamed violently.

"It wasn't there, I tell you. Hollis must have stashed it," Gage said, coughing up blood.

Mr. B shook his head. "I thought you were done lying to me, Gage. My own face is starting to hurt just looking at you," he chuckled. Turning to Slick, he said, "I'm hungry. Any of you guys hungry? How about some nice roast beef, huh?" Turning to eye Gage again, he leaned in close and said, "I've got my own slicer, you know."

Mr. B stood back and pointed to the bar. Sure enough, a deli meat slicer was sitting on the counter, gleaming menacingly under the bar's bare bulbs.

"It's cheaper that way," Mr. B explained lightly, "and besides, I get to slice it just the way I like it. How do you like yours, Gage? Fat? Lean? I can do it any way you like. I've had lots of practice."

Gage stared at the meat slicer, his knees starting to go weak. His eyes widened in fear as Mr. B motioned to Slick. "Go turn it on," he said. "I want to show Gage how it works."

Slick sneered and went over to flip on the slicer's switch. The blade whirred to life, metal ominously spinning in the guide.

Mr. B walked over to the slicer, inspecting it with conceit. "Better bring him over here so he can get a closer look," he ordered, as JT and Tyrone dragged Gage across the floor toward the bar. Gage began to struggle in their grasp but went limp after Crusher whacked the back of his neck with the butt of a .45.

The two men hauled Gage over and Slick stretched his arm out so that Gage's hand was only inches away from the spinning, razor-sharp blade.

"What's it gonna be, Gage?" Mr. B threatened. "Fat or lean?"

Gage's hand was brought closer to the slicer. Groggy and panic-stricken, he couldn't even struggle under the weight of the four men holding him down. In horror, he watched as his hand was brought close enough to the slicer that he felt the air blown by the whizzing blade.

Just as his fingertip was nicked, Gage yelled out. "Alright, alright! I took the money!"

Mr. B advanced threateningly. "I know you took the money, Gage. What did you do with it?"

"I was using it to make an album with Diamond," Gage blurted out.

"Now why didn't you say that in the first place?" Mr. B said, all smiles now as he switched off the slicer. Gage was able to withdraw his hand from the blade. "Did you think I wasn't ever going to find out?" Mr. B continued, the venom back in his voice.

Gage lifted up his head and slowly wiped the blood from his mouth. "I'm tellin' you, Mr. B, I didn't know Hollis worked for you."

"I'm sure you didn't. But two weeks ago, right here in my office, I told you that somebody jacked Hollis and took my twenty grand. Why didn't you come clean then, huh? All you had to say was, 'I'm awfully sorry, Mr. B. I took your money, and here all of it is,' " Mr. B drawled sarcastically.

"I was afraid that . . ." Gage began, but he began to cough again, bringing up more blood.

"Afraid, huh? So afraid that you were out spending my money, playing yourself off as some hot-shot music producer." Mr. B mopped his fat neck with the clean side of his handkerchief and shook his head. "I told Diamond he should have gotten himself a real manager, not some two-bit hood like you. Now look at the shit you got him into."

Gage suddenly sat upright. "Look, Diamond had nothing to do with this. I did Hollis alone. I didn't even tell Diamond where I got the money."

Mr. B narrowed his eyes. "Well, maybe he should have asked before he started to spend other people's money."

"I'll get you your money back, Mr. B. I swear it," Gage said solemnly.

Mr. B nodded, then paused, scratching his chin. After thinking for a few moments, he said, "This album of Diamond's. Is it any good?"

Gage looked around at Mr. B and his cronies,

who were grinning evilly. Tyronne and Slick often came to the Hip Hop Emporium and had heard Diamond rap before during Open Mic Nite. He could see the gleam in their eyes, sizing themselves up as music producers, already planning their pick-up lines for ladies at the club.

Gage could see where Mr. B was going with this and he didn't like it. Sure, he himself was no manager, but he did come up with the cash for his homey. And Diamond would be famous one day, of that Gage was sure. There was no way these weasels, even Mr. B, were going to take the profits for themselves.

"Look, Mr. B, this is between you and me. Leave Diamond out of it," Gage said evenly.

Mr. B just leaned back, placing his hands on his fat belly. "I always did want to get into the music industry," he said. "Who knows? Maybe this is a blessing in disguise. Maybe being a producer will be a welcome change from this hole. I'm getting kind of tired of the company, anyway," he added, looking disdainfully at his men, who were practically salivating at the prospect of getting in on the action.

Gage figured there was nothing he could do; Mr. B was involved now. "Look, I'll get you double your money back, Mr. B. Just let us finish up the album."

"I'll tell you what," said Mr. B, leaning forward. "If I like the album, I'll call it an even trade."

"You can't do that!" Gage shouted.

"Don't tell me what I can or can't do, boy. You're lucky that I don't kill you right here!" Mr.

B shot back. He turned to Crusher and Slick. "Get rid of him. Tyrone, JT, you two come with me. Let's go see our friend Diamond," he said.

Crusher stood up, grabbing Gage by his ripped shirt collar. Flashing him a sadistic grin, Crusher hauled Gage backward into the club's back room.

Diamond sat behind the wheel of the Cutlass, with Tamara right beside him riding shotgun. They were on their way to the studio to tell Cliff the good news—they were going to get married. In the morning, when Diamond woke up beside Tamara, he felt that a change had come over him, somehow. As he rolled over and watched Tamara sleep, her chest softly rising and falling, he knew that he wanted to wake up this way, every morning, for the rest of his life.

He kissed Tamara on the cheek, and she twitched adorably in her sleep. Diamond got up quietly and started breakfast, just like he had for his mother. He prepared it skillfully, and it was done in only a few minutes. Placing a plate of food on a service tray, Diamond walked back into the bedroom, waking his lover up with another kiss.

Tamara adored the fact that Diamond was serving her breakfast in bed. She gleamed when he presented her with a paper rose he made from a napkin. And she shouted out with joy when he knelt down beside the bed and proposed. The two had spent the rest of the morning making love. They devoured each other in bliss, never wanting the moment to end.

Later, in the car, Tamara turned excitedly toward Diamond. "What do you think your father is going to say?"

"He's cool. He knows how I feel about you and stuff."

"Yeah, but do you think he'll suppose it's just because I'm pregnant?"

"He'll probably be wondering why I didn't ask you to marry me sooner," Diamond said, reaching over and squeezing Tamara's hand.

Tamara smiled broadly, squeezing back. As they drove down the street, Tamara kept smiling, continuing to watch her man's profile as he guided the huge car toward the traffic lights.

Gage slumped in a chair, his breath shallow. Slick and Crusher stood over him, laughing. "Yo," Crusher said, "you still alive, Gage?" This cracked both of them up some more.

When their laughter finally died down, Slick asked, "So, what are we gonna do with him?"

Crusher shrugged. "Mr. B said to get rid of him."

"Does that mean we're supposed to kill him, or what?" asked Slick, looking like he'd enjoy it if they did.

Crusher's face drew a blank. "Uh, I don't know. He wasn't specific." The two faced each other silently. "So what do we do?"

Slick thought about it for a second. "If we let him go and Mr. B wanted him dead, we'll be in serious fucking trouble. But if Mr. B was gonna let him live and we killed him, I don't think

Mr. B will give a fuck, do you? So if we kill him, we can't lose!"

Crusher's eyes brightened. "You're right. Let's take him out back," he said eagerly, and reached down to lift Gage up from the chair in a fireman's carry.

As he did, Gage noticed a flash by Crusher's feet. When the big man leaned over, his pant leg rose up, revealing a Saturday night special tucked into a black ankle holster.

Even in Gage's dizzy haze, his own words came back to him. He recalled back to when he was playing around with Diamond outside of Marshall's studio, the night he got bumped by Master Mix. *Never know when a little gun like this is gonna save your life*, he had said.

Crusher had already grabbed Gage by the neck, forcing his head down so he could sling Gage's body over his shoulder. In that moment, Gage's head and arm dangled by Crusher's feet, and in an instant, Gage reached down and ripped the gun from the ankle holster.

Crusher, who was half-bent, knew something had happened when he felt a tug on his foot. But not until Gage had pushed away from him, sticking a gun in his gut, did he know just how bad the situation was. And by then it was too late.

Gage fired off a shot and Crusher immediately hunched over, his hands flying to his belly. Looking at the blood pumping out from beneath his fingers, he charged at Gage. Gage stood and fired twice, hitting him in the chest before Crusher's bulk finally fell.

As Crusher went down, Gage looked over to Slick, who had already drawn a nine millimeter and was just now swinging it around toward him. Slick started blasting as Gage dove to the floor, grabbing Crusher by the lapels. With tremendous effort, he hoisted the big man off the floor, using him as a shield as he advanced toward Slick. Bullets tore into Crusher's back, ripping apart his jacket and splattering blood on them both.

The concussions knocked Crusher's body forward, and as he fell again, Gage stepped back and fired three times in quick succession. Two bullets erupted Slick's chest. The third hit him right between the eyes.

Slick dropped on the spot, his gun clattering to the floor in front of him. Gage didn't waste a second. He grabbed both guns and bolted out of the club. Getting into his Bronco, he turned the ignition, stomped on the gas, and peeled away.

Cliff sat in front of the piano, playing bittersweet jazz. The way he was completely immersed in the music, he could have been the only person in the entire world. His long agile fingers stroked the ivories, making the piano hum. Music made Cliff feel complete. And as he improvised high into the scale, Cliff lost himself in the song, painting a picture with sound.

The low booming bass notes were like storm clouds gathering, darkening the horizon. High glissandos were like the rain, beating down on soft earth. He used the pedals to give vibrato to the tenor notes, making them sound like flashes of lightning. And as Cliff played out the tempest in his soul, Marshall watched from the doorway, his hands quietly folded in front of him.

Cliff's song took a turn from its torrid jazz riffs and settled down into a soft melody. As he ended, Marshall clapped behind him.

"Don't your fingers ever get tired?" he laughed, walking to the piano and clasping Cliff's shoulder.

Cliff laughed. "Uh-uh. I'm just making up for lost time, that's all."

"It's getting on, Cliff. Do you need a ride home?"

"Nah, Diamond should be here any minute. He said he had some news for me." Just then, the lobby's doorbell sounded. "Speak of the devil," said Cliff, putting the keyguard down over the piano.

"I'll go tell him you're in here," said Marshall as he turned and left the studio, walking down the hall toward the lobby.

As he turned the corner and walked past the lobby desk, Marshall saw three men standing there, looking threatening. One was older and had a sharp suit on, with a walking cane. Marshall had dealt with all types, both inside and outside of his studio, and whoever these guys were he wasn't going to be intimidated.

"What do you guys want? I'm closed for the night."

Mr. B stepped forward. "I'm looking for Diamond St. James."

"He's not here," replied Marshall, crossing his thick arms.

"You run this place?" asked Mr. B, running a gloved hand over the lobby's Sherwood desk.

"Yeah, this is my studio."

"That's nice," said Mr. B. "I like to see a brother in business for himself." Marshall wondered exactly what kind of business these guys were in.

Cliff walked into the lobby. Marshall turned to him, saying, "These gentlemen are looking for Diamond."

Cliff sensed something was up. "What do you want with him?" he asked Mr. B, immediately recognizing that he was the ringleader in this posse.

"And who are you?" asked Mr. B disdainfully.

"I'm his father," replied Cliff strictly.

"Well, your boy owes me twenty grand."

Cliff was stunned. "How is it he owes you that kind of money?" he asked.

"That's between him and I," replied Mr. B, removing his gloves. With JT and Tyrone glaring after him, Mr. B walked past Marshall and Cliff and down the hall, toward the studio. Marshall and Cliff looked at each other with concern in their eyes and followed them.

In the control room, Mr. B looked around, surveying the mixing board. Turning a few knobs and flipping a couple of switches, he swung around to face Marshall.

"Nice setup you got going on here," he said. "I don't know much about the music business, but this stuff looks first rate. You must have, what, a couple hundred thousand tied up with all this fancy equipment?"

Marshall didn't reply, nervously glancing back and forth at Mr. B's roving hands and at his henchmen's sly smiles.

"I want to make this real simple for you," Mr. B continued. "Time is money and money is time— I know you can appreciate that because you're in the record business. All I want is Diamond's master disks."

Marshall held firm. "That's out of the question. I can't give you that—they're his property."

"No, they're mine. They belong to me now," said Mr. B, ending the discussion. Cliff couldn't hold himself back any longer. There was no way this gangster was taking Diamond's master away. He had worked too hard for it. They all had, for that matter.

Cliff took a step toward Mr. B, but Tyrone quickly grabbed his arm. "This ain't any of your business, pop," he breathed into Cliff's face.

Mr. B figured he had waited long enough. He motioned over to JT, who pulled out a nine millimeter from a shoulder holster and pointed it directly at Marshall's head.

"Get the master. Now!" Mr. B shouted.

Marshall backed away slowly. "Okay, chill. The disks are in my office."

"Go with him," Mr. B told JT. "If he tries anything—and I mean anything—shoot the motherfucker dead."

Marshall stepped into his office, with a gun at his back. He began to walk around his desk when

JT stopped him. "Hey old man, where you think you're going?"

"The disks are locked up in that cabinet. I need the keys to open it," Marshall replied.

"Well, hurry up and be quick about it. I ain't got a lot of time, here, so just open the fucking thing."

"Keys are in the desk," Marshall said, leaning over and opening up the top drawer. Glancing down, he saw the only two items in it—a ring of keys and a .35. His hand wavered over the gun, and as JT began to suspiciously walk over, Marshall grabbed the keys and quickly slammed the drawer closed.

Walking over to the cabinet, Marshall inserted a key into the lock and opened the sliding door. Taking a plastic case with two master disks in it from inside, Marshall crossed his office and handed the case to JT.

"Well, that was easy, wasn't it?" said JT. Waving his gun, JT motioned Marshall toward the door.

Diamond pulled up in the studio parking lot and practically leaped out of the car. He circled around the hood and opened the door for Tamara with an exaggerated bow, like a Plaza Hotel doorman. Giggling, Tamara slid out of the car, curtseying politely. Diamond kissed her, and the two headed up the stairs into the studio's lobby.

The chimes tingled as they walked through the door. "Yo, anybody there?" Diamond called down the hall. "Marshall? Cliff?"

"Oh, they're here alright," replied a voice behind them. Diamond spun around and came face to face with Tyrone, who was pointing a Glock at his head. Enraged, Diamond started to charge forward.

"Uh, uh, uh, Diamond. Have patience," said Tyrone, calmly aiming at Tamara. "We don't want to do anything rash, now, would we? You make a move, and I'll blow both of your motherfucking heads off. Her first, you later," he leered.

Diamond froze, seething in anger. His fists clenched by his side, Diamond knew Tyrone wasn't kidding. Hell, he had seen Tyrone blow people away with his own two eyes. The brother had no fear.

Mr. B stepped into the lobby from the hallway. "Well, well, it's Diamond, the ghetto superstar. What's shaking, D?" he jeered arrogantly.

"What's going on, Mr. B?" Diamond demanded.

"I came to collect my money. Or didn't your 'manager' tell you who generously leant him the funds to let you record your record?" he said.

Diamond stiffened. "I don't know nothing about your money."

Mr. B cocked an eyebrow. "Funny, that's the same thing Gage said, until I applied some pressure, that is," he smiled cruelly.

Mr. B pulled a silver-plated gun with ebony grips out of his jacket and pointed it at Diamond. Along with Tyrone, Mr. B hustled Diamond and a frightened Tamara down the hallway toward the studio.

*   *   *

Because his left collarbone was broken, Gage couldn't lift his left arm. He had to wrench the wheel of the Bronco, which was now hurtling down back streets at full speed, with only one hand. Sweat poured off his brow, stinging his eyes. One side of his face puffed out, and his mouth bled freely.

Swerving wildly, and almost skidding through a fence, Gage drove over a lawn, knocking recycling bins everywhere in a shower of glass. Just as he regained control of the Bronco, a cat streaked out in the middle of the street. Swearing, Gage jerked the wheel to the right, barely missing a telephone pole but running over several parking meters. He bounced back onto the road, his tires screeching.

A rim popped and the forward right tire went out. The Bronco's front end dropped forward as the rear began to fishtail. Sparks showered the windshield as Gage struggled to regain control of the vehicle. Finally, Gage pulled into the studio's parking lot, the ride a smoking wreck.

Dragging himself out of the car, he lurched toward the front steps. As he did, he saw two men with guns through the lobby's large picture windows. Stumbling closer, Gage recognized Mr. B, a cane in one hand and a gun in the other, leading Diamond down the hallway toward the studio.

"Shit."

"Let's go, pops. I said move." JT raised his gun to eye level, his thumb tilted inward and down.

Marshall stayed put, his mind racing. If he

could just make it to the desk, he might be able to take this punk out. As a vet, he was trained to kill. A professional. But he needed his tools. There was no training for what to do when a gun is aimed directly at your defenseless head.

"I ain't gonna say it one more time, now move," JT yelled.

Marshall began to move past his desk, toward JT and the door, when JT grabbed him by the scruff of the neck and hurled him onto the floor.

"Ha! Get off yo' ass, old man. You may talk tough, but you're feeble. Now let's go!" JT heartlessly laughed and raised his leg to deliver a kick to Marshall's stomach.

It was just the chance Marshall needed. Still on the ground, he lashed out with his foot, sweeping JT's other leg from underneath him and sending him sprawling to the floor. JT landed hard on his ass with a look of surprise on his face.

In a flash, Marshall was around the front of his desk and had the drawer open. JT was already raising his piece, aiming dead center at Marshall's chest. Marshall grabbed his revolver, dove sideways, and fired as he fell.

JT's body jerked back with each shot. Wide, gaping, bloody holes tattooed his torso as six slugs pounded into him in tight formation. With a look of shock on his face, JT's gun went off reflexively. The shot careened wide, hitting a sheaf of music paper and sending pages fluttering to the floor.

Marshall stood up slowly. "Got you motherfucker."

* * *

When the shots went off, Tamara shrieked. Diamond gave her a determined look. Mr. B dropped his cane and shoved his gun up against the back of Diamond's head. "Careful, boy, careful. You don't want to do nothing stupid now, do you? Isn't that right, Tyrone?"

Tyrone grabbed Tamara by her hair and raised a Glock to her chin.

"Stop!" Diamond yelled. "Let's everyone relax here."

"That's a good idea Diamond. Let's all just take a breath and review the situation," Mr. B said. "Tyrone, go check out Marshall's office. Shoot anything that moves. I'll keep watch over the young lovers."

The hallway was silent when Tyrone went out. "JT? Wassup?" he called.

No one answered him. The corridor remained as silent as the soundproof recording booths.

Mr. B kept one eye on Tamara and Diamond and one on Tyrone. Had he known to use his third eye correctly, he would have seen Gage, battered and bleeding, walking through the lobby's door.

Gage got a bead on Mr. B's shiny black head with his .09.

Getting inside of Marshall's office, Tyrone saw JT lying in a pool of blood. He couldn't see Marshall, who quickly let off two bad shots. Tyrone deduced the vet's position and swept the office with his full clip. Marshall was blasted from his feet and came down with a loud crunch. His lungs were both punctured. Blood bubbled in his mouth.

The last image he would see was a gold record hanging on the wall, shining like a twelve-inch sun.

Gage missed the gangster's head by centimeters. Mr. B ducked, then tore down the hallway as he heard Tryone's clip emptying. Gage tossed his .09 to Diamond and pulled a .45 from his waist as they went down the hall—Gage with a limp, Diamond with a stride—to get Mr. B.

Cliff's hand just hung up the phone with the authorities when the skinny gangster skidded into the control room. By the time Gage and Diamond got into the room, Mr. B was aiming squarely at the old musician's head.

Diamond ran in, hammer cocked at Mr. B's head.

Gage followed shortly thereafter.

Then came Tyrone with a fresh clip of bullets and a whimpering Tamara.

It was a standoff. No one dared move an inch.

Most surprisingly, Mr. B was nervous. Sweat glistened on his brow; his eyes darted around maniacally. Gage peered at him closely, his bruised arm wavering with the weight of his weapon, and crept forward.

"Easy, now, Gage. You don't want this man to die," Mr. B said, jutting his gun at Cliff.

"He ain't *my* father."

Mr. B watched closely as a slow smile spread across Gage's bloody face. Mr. B guaranteed Cliff a death certificate with a clean head shot, then swung and fired at the boy he raised like a son.

It was all hell broken loose—blasts and flashes, like the Fourth of July. Glass shattered, equipment sparked.

Diamond spun and laid Tyrone to rest with six shots to the chest.

Gage caught two in his abdomen and returned the favor with three slugs into Mr. B's shoulder. The crime lord was blown back against the console. Stunned from the blow, he was unable to do anything but smile when Gage walked over and spread his brains across a wall of audio equipment.

Then, as soon as it erupted, everything broke quiet, leaving thick clouds of smoke and dead bodies as evidence as to what had happened.

AMAZING GRACE

"Ashes to ashes, dust to dust . . ."

The preacher finished the ceremony, and for the second time in what seemed like days, Diamond shoveled dirt onto the coffin of one of his parents.

Another gloomy day, another small affair. A few of Cliff's friends, musicians who played on Diamond's album, attended the somber funeral, telling stories about Cliff in his heydey after the service. The preacher, a diminutive man named Jones, wished Diamond and Tamara well and walked them to the Cutlass. They had already signed on as members of his church and planned to have their wedding ceremony there in a few weeks.

"Diamond, I hope with all of the tragedy in your recent past, you find strength in the Lord, and your beautiful bride to be."

"Thanks for everything, brother Jones. Can I get back to you next week about paying for the services?"

"Yes, my son, take your time, get your affairs

in order. I can always take up a collection to help you out in the meantime. You call me if you need anything, you hear?"

Diamond smiled. "Thanks, brother, I appreciate it." With Tamara smiling at him warmly from the front seat, Diamond pulled the Cutlass out of the cemetery and drove into their future.

Michael lay in a hospital bed under twenty-four-hour police protection and was allowed no visitors.

A large record label wound up buying Marshall's studio. They planned to restore the entire interior, even the gold records on the walls, in honor of Marshall.

As workers swept up the rooms, cleaning up the broken glass and chunks of plaster, record executives were taking a tour of the facilities.

"Is it true that people died here?" one executive asked.

A young associate scurried around, trying to make the rubble look somewhat presentable. "Yes, well why do you think we were able to pick up the mortgage on this place so cheap?"

The young man swept some plaster underneath the console. "Just look at this equipment," he beamed. "Except for the mixing board which was ruined beyond repair, it's all in prime condition."

The executives milled about the studio, checking out the setup. Most began adding figures in their heads, trying to calculate the immediate profit they would make on the place. A few were already thinking about the potential for franchises in inner cities.

But one of them bent down, his gaze setting on a set of master reels on the floor. Wiping it off with his handkerchief, he took a closer look at the label. "Who is Diamond St. James?" he asked.

"No one I've ever heard of," scoffed the young associate.

"Well, do me a favor—cue this up. Let's have a listen to this 'Ghetto Supastar.' "